INCA SUN

By DAVID BLACK

INCA SUN

Copyright © David Black 2013

Published on Kindle format by David Black Books 2013
Published in Paperback by David Black Books 2013

ISBN: 13-978-1492164869
ISBN: 10-1492164860

Cover design: David Black Books
☐

2

Dedication:

To my dearest mother, Olive; a remarkable and most wonderful lady. Her sudden passing has saddened so many, who loved her so much.

'The stars have dimmed, mum x'

* * *

With grateful thanks to Trev and Elaine Hall for their generous assistance in the proof-reading stage before publication

Other great books by David Black:

Siege of Faith
Chronicles of Sir Richard Starkey #1

Eagles of the Damned
Roman Legion Series #1

The Great Satan
(Shadow Squadron #1)

Dark Empire
(Shadow Squadron #2)

Playing for England

For more information visit:
http://www.davidblackbooks.com

Forward
Part 1

* * *

Spain
Anno Domini -1568

Long ago, in the year 1568, the Spanish Empire of his most Catholic majesty, King Phillip II, continued to grow and prosper. Following the abdication of his father, the glittering renaissance of the Spanish Crown was fuelled by vast quantities of gold, silver and precious stones, torn from the dark earth of his recently inherited South American colonies.

Free at last of the mosquito ridden ports of the New World, under sails of canvas emblazoned with the Holy Cross, great convoys of wooden treasure galleons sailed ponderously eastwards across the mighty Atlantic Ocean, under the protection of the Spanish King's banner, and his heavily armed naval escorts.

Providing luck and the blessed Madonna were with them, Phillip's ships would make landfall on the Iberian Peninsula close to the Spanish port of Cadiz, after a long and perilous passage. If their Captain's successfully avoided roaming pirates and treacherous and capricious ocean storms, Royal patronage and considerable reward awaited those whose treasure ships arrived safely in Spanish waters; their cavernous holds gorged with heavy ingots of gold, silver and fortunes of looted Aztec, Mayan and Inca treasure.

Vain, bigoted and ambitious, King Phillip's commands to seek out ever more land and riches left no room for doubt or ambiguity in the minds of his distant soldiers. Spurred on by Royal edict and their own lust for gold and fortune, the

Conquistadors plunged deeper into the steaming jungles and crossed great mountain ranges in their search for new South American territories. Engineers quickly followed, and expanded intensive mining operations close behind the invaders, as the cruel Spaniard's remorseless advance continued.

As a consequence of their mining, the New World's Spanish Governors needed native labour to toil through day and night in the dank bowels of the unforgiving earth. Flint tipped arrows; stone axes and suicidal courage was no match for scything grapeshot and Spanish heavy cavalry. Entire villages were systematically surrounded and cleared of their populations; survivors were ruthlessly enslaved by the heavily armed, cold-hearted white men from far across the sea.

Manacled and marched into hopeless slavery, scant regard to the well-being of the latest subjects of the Spaniard King was paid by Conquistador nobles. Avarice and expediency governed treatment of common slaves. Captive men, women and children often went unprotected from the excesses of their cruel iron-shirted masters, in the hidden depths of both misty mountain and steaming jungle.

As the Spanish invasion of South America continued on a course of rapid expansion, the ancient Mayan, Inca and Aztec civilizations were decimated; their people mercilessly lashed, tortured and worked to death, to feed their wholly indifferent overlord's insatiable lust for riches; ripped by starving, exhausted slaves from the dark and claustrophobic mines of Mexico and Peru.

* * *

When stories of fabulous riches were told; gossip of King Phillip's burgeoning wealth spread quickly through the Royal Courts of Europe. Portugal was first to seize the moment, sending ships of expedition, laden with navigators and adventures, whose sole aim was, in the name of their sovereign, to claim vast tracts of land which the Spaniards had not yet exploited in the New World.

* * *

Part 2

* * *

England
Anno Domini -1568

1568 was a turbulent year for England's people, and for their young Queen. It was the ninth year of her reign, since she had assumed the Tudor throne, following the death of her devout and tyrannical Catholic half-sister, Bloody Mary.

Threatened by a background of Catholic plots, and a myriad of European enemies, England's Queen Elizabeth had also listened with great interest to the stories of glittering fortunes, which were the height of gossip among the aristocratic courtiers who thronged her Royal Court. Circumstances, however, dictated she must take a different approach to tales of fabulous wealth, which emanated from the Spanish Court in Madrid. Short of gold to fund the acquisition of uncertain lands, Elizabeth sought older avenues to snatch a share of the bounty. Lack of resources forced England's sovereign to switch her attention from conquering distant lands, looking instead to the dazzling riches locked inside the holds of the treasure ships, wallowing across the wide Atlantic Ocean, sailing slowly towards her bitterest enemies: King Phillip, and the Catholic Empire of Spain.

During those dark and turbulent days, other weighty concerns cast ominous shadows across Protestant England's horizons, and were never far from the young Queen's thoughts. With the huge influx of gold into Phillip's treasury, Elizabeth's spies and her own powerful intellect quickly defined that armed conflict with Catholic Spain was inevitable.

The seeds of war were sown by her late father, Henry VIII. Denied a Papal divorce from his first wife, the outraged King Henry seized the assets of the Catholic churches within his realm. Under Royal proclamation, his stringent Reformation began. Valuable lands were confiscated; Abbeys, Priories and Convents were ruthlessly looted and stripped of their wealth. The excommunicated King now declared spiritual independence from Rome, and promoted himself head of the new Church of England.

As Henry grew rich from his legacy of ecclesiastical plunder, the relationship between Catholic Spain and Protestant England rapidly deteriorated; mutual mistrust and bitter religious hatred deepened as quickly as the political gap widened between them.

Barely tolerated in the Spanish Court, the English Ambassador regularly sent secret messages to Elizabeth's spy master, Sir Francis Walsingham. As his worried eyes scanned the Ambassador's latest dispatches, Sir Frances' concerns grew exponentially with each new line he read…

'Once Phillip's mighty Armada has crushed Queen Elizabeth's navy off England's southerly shores, thousands of Spanish foot soldiers and heavy armoured cavalry, who sailed with the Armada from Spain, or were embarked from his Dutch dominions, will land on the shores of Kent and Norfolk. From captured southern and eastern beaches, England's Conquistadores will then begin their triumphant march towards London…'

8

Phillip gloated with his generals and admirals, during regular meetings to discuss the progress of shipbuilding for the coming invasion. They exulted together at the thought of the uncivilised and piratical English becoming little more than slaves of the ever expanding, and ruthlessly controlled Catholic empire.

Once conquered and their spirit broken, England's heretic people, who betrayed even the slightest reluctance to shed their Protestant blasphemy and re-embrace Catholicism, were to be converted back into the arms of the one true Church by the cruel and fanatical priests of Phillip's dreaded Inquisition, using fire and thumbscrew, where threats and coercion had failed. Inevitably, most noble English families would become his vassals. Others would simply be lost within the turbulent swirl of an uncertain future.

Despite recent increases of overseas trade in English wool, Elizabeth's treasury continued to teeter on the verge of bankruptcy. Even with her best efforts to correct the shortfalls, it stubbornly remained almost empty.

To help fill her near bankrupt treasury, she had ordered new overseas markets to be exploited, and older commercial partners pressured to increase trade with her English merchant fleet. Recent sales of valuable cannon and wool to Spain's Muslim foe in the east, the powerful Ottoman Empire, had helped considerably to keep Elizabeth's creditors at bay, but at best, it was only a temporary reprieve.

One profound advantage Elizabeth had to protect her small island kingdom was the watery redoubt of the English Channel, and her reservoir of brave and daring sea captains. She knew that when the Spanish invasion fleet finally sailed, the tactical flair and courage of men like Howard, Drake and

9

Frobisher would be the backbone of her naval defence. They had sailed the coasts of England since boyhood, and would use the capricious winds and tides to their advantage when the time came.

There were other newer captains too, who had also gained favour at Court in the past few years. One such brave knight was Sir Richard Starkey, who had served as the Queen's agent on Malta, during the great Ottoman siege several years previously. He had made a formal report to her on his return to England's shores that huge amounts of military ordinance had been lost or abandoned when the Turks were broken and soundly beaten at the walls of Malta's Christian fortresses, after five months of the bloody Ottoman's siege.

Grasping the opportunity to beat her European enemies to the prize, Elizabeth immediately ordered a flotilla of merchant ships, laden with English cannon, to be dispatched. Unfortunately, during their long sea voyage to Constantinople, the old friend of England, Ottoman Caliph Suleiman the Magnificent died. When the English ships eventually anchored in the Byzantine waters of the Bosphorus, they found to their dismay that the new Caliph's armament procurers already knew of England's trading predicament and drove ever harder bargains for the prized English cannon, before parting with their Sultan's Muslim gold.

While England's merchant marine remained strong, her navy's sailors often went unpaid for months, and her warships lay mostly rotting at anchor in poorly maintained condition. Elizabeth realised that to make repairs, and build a new generation of stout ships to defend her island kingdom; she needed money. With the threat of Spanish invasion only a few short years away, she needed it quickly. Her Privy Council's suggestion of gathering yet more taxes on the heavily burdened people of England was angrily rejected by their fiery red-haired monarch. There was quite enough political plotting and religious turmoil permeating her kingdom already.

Danger and intrigue lurked everywhere. On her northern border, the staunchly Catholic Scottish Queen Mary continued to flirt with France. To the west, across the Irish Sea, swirling mist-filled bogs sucked down her soldiers sent to quell constant Celtic rebellion. The North Sea offered a measure of protection from thousands of Spanish troops permanently stationed within the Spanish King's colony of the Netherlands. Thankfully, under the command of the merciless Duke of Alva, the battle-hardened Spanish soldiers and Phillip's legion of foreign mercenaries were kept busy putting down constant insurrection by the Calvinist Hollanders, who wished to shed the brutal oppression of the Spanish yoke and the Catholic Church. Despite the new menace of Phillip's Armada, King Phillip's mailed fist beyond the narrow straits of the stormy North Sea remained a dangerous and permanent threat to England's shores.

Elizabeth's Tudor blood made her an astute ruler. She quickly divined, since her coronation, that to remain monarch and avoid full-blown civil war from her many Catholic nobles and subjects, she desperately needed the support of all her common people. Recent bad weather and failed harvests made life for her people especially difficult. Burdening them with more crippling taxes was not the way to foster the love, admiration and loyalty they had shown her so far during her short and turbulent reign.

After many long and gloomy meetings, and countless hours of deliberation and heated discussion, the last of her Privy Councillors suggestions for new ways to raise money were exhausted. Only one highly dangerous path remained open to Elizabeth. Filled with foreboding, her councillors reluctantly suggested that perhaps fresh Letters of Marque might secretly be issued.

Since the distant time of King Henry III, although angrily denied to outraged foreign ambassadors, it was a highly lucrative practice within the shadows of the English Court to issue Letters of Reprisal. Such documents were delivered by trusted hand to the monarch's most daring sea captains. The Letters were a licence of freedom to attack foreign ships on the high seas, without fear of punishment under English piracy laws, provided the Crown had its share of the booty.

Letters of Reprisal were the precursor to the more wide-ranging Letters of Marque, which when adorned with the monarch's own great seal, gave chosen captains free rein to wage war on alien merchant vessels. The Letters were surreptitiously granted to loyal and trusted privateers in later centuries; men who knew when to keep their gun ports open, and their mouths firmly shut.

On the evening tide, looted cargos were quietly returned to England's seaports. As darkness fell, the booty disappeared forever, having been sold to equally unscrupulous merchants within hours of arrival at English harbours. Profits were quietly absorbed into the Royal coffers, while smaller percentages disappeared into the captain's private purses.

When debate was over, and Royal agreement finally sanctioned, the Privy Council's business was concluded for the day. The Queen's noble advisors bowed low and respectfully withdrew. Elizabeth was left alone in the quiet and reflective solitude of her private audience chamber. Within the great fireplace, flames crackled and sparks flared inside the oak panelled Stateroom, as they struggled to warm the chill of the wet afternoon outside. The Queen stared gloomily at the dancing sparks. Their flickering glow did nothing to lift the feeling of cold despair which enveloped her. With hands clasped tightly together, she paced slowly away from the warmth of the fire, towards the largest of the great bay windows.

Outside, Hampton Court's orderly gardens glistened in the falling rain. With unseeing eyes, the Queen wrestled with the decision she must soon make. Should things go badly, she thought, the Letters of Marque could well trigger early war with Spain, for which her nation was desperately ill-prepared. Wringing her bejewelled hands, Elizabeth turned away from the vista of her ornate gardens. She began to slowly pace back and forth. What else could she do, she fretted, but sign and seal the wretched Letters?

Her spies hinted that Phillip's plans of invasion offered at best only a few short years' grace, before the great Armada was fully commissioned and ready to set sail for England.

Elizabeth was well aware that her own future as Queen, and the very survival of her nation would soon balance on the success and daring of a handful of her bravest captains; men she prayed would bring their resolute courage to her table, and answer England's call, to what would certainly be her realm's darkest hour.

With a deep sigh, Elizabeth abruptly stopped her nervous pacing beside the great bay window. Her gaze slowly shifted beyond the ornate flower beds, dripping roofs and drenched spires of her palace, towards the dark clouds on the brooding western horizon. She stared silently through the falling rain as she contemplated the terrible gamble to which she must now commit England's future. To save her realm, Elizabeth knew she had no alternative. She must stake her future on looting at least part of the fabulous wealth that sailed across the cold grey waters of the Atlantic; riches destined for the avaricious clutches of England's greatest enemy…

Chapter One

On broad obsidian wings, the great Condor drifted silently across the heavens, as it rode on an invisible and powerful updraft. The intense up-swelling of air, which lifted its heavy body, was driven by clashing warm air from the vast, untamed Mexican jungle, colliding with damp cooler air, blowing inshore from the grey expanse of the mighty Atlantic Ocean.

Senses alert, the great bird wheeled and spiralled at the very edge of its vast hunting territory through a bright and cloudless sky. The old vulture had not fed for days; hunger gnawed at its empty belly. The carrion eater searched patiently for sight or smell of the rotting flesh or putrid fish on which it would usually feast. Far below, beyond the foaming coastline, the immense ocean's waters sparkled and danced, scored with endless rows of white capped waves. Unusually on its lonely patrol, the hungry bird spied something strange in the waters far below…

'Steady as she goes, Will!'

Standing on the Sea Hawk's creaking quarterdeck, beneath billowing sails and the same blue skies, the privateer's first officer nodded acknowledgement of his Captain's order.

'Aye Sir… Steady as she goes.'

Two full-rigged ships ploughed under every ounce of sail their complicated lattice of rigging could carry. Across the surface of the sparkling ocean, tall wooden masts groaned and creaked as moisture laden trade winds filled straining sails, fuelling the pursuit and propelling both ships through the empty waters of the Yucatan Peninsula.

The ship now pursuing him, less than half a league off the merchantman's stern, was the blood-curdling spectre dreaded by all Spanish merchant ships, sailing alone and unprotected along the deserted coastline of the New World. Staining under full sail, his pursuer was an English privateer, intent on chasing down the fat Spanish galleon and capturing it as a valuable prize for his distant heretic Queen.

The Spanish vessel's crew had been working frantically, in a state of near panic, throughout the long hot morning, as they tried everything to coax more speed from their heavily laden ship. The frenetic crewmen were well aware their chances of survival were slim at best, if the English pirate caught up with them, alone as they were, on the open lonely seas.

The sinister grey spectre had been closing on the Spaniard since dawn.

At first, hours earlier, the Spaniard's master had breathed a sigh of profound relief. He assumed the tall masts of the distant ship to be one of his own scattered flotilla. However, as the sun-burnt off the sea mist and visibility gradually improved, a sharp-eyed lookout, high in the Santa Juliana's rigging, quickly changed joy to horror when the seaman desperately screamed down a warning. His sharp eyes had detected the hated English flag of St. George flying from the closing ship's stern.

Heavily laden, the galleon was sluggish to the helm and riding low in the water. Experience from years at sea told the Spanish captain he had but one chance, and that, at best, offered meagre hope of salvation. If only, he thought desperately, he could outrun the privateer and reach the safety of the small inlet of Anton Lizardo, just twenty nautical miles further along the sandy strip of coastline, which separated the lush jungle cloaked mainland, from the vast empty ocean. The inlet he sought lay to the northwest of the port of Boca Del Rio, close to the nearby provincial capital of Veracruz. Tightly clutching his rosary, he lifted it to his lips as he offered up a silent prayer to all the holy Saints, that there would indeed be Spanish warships anchored in the inlet. They were the King's escort waiting for the treasure

15

convoy, when it was fully assembled. If he was right, their guns would protect him from the English pirate closing fast off his stern.

The simple truth was bleak, however. Even as the merchantman's hour-glass slowly emptied under the dazzling glare of the sun; his chances of outrunning his pursuer diminished with the fall of each tiny grain of sand.

When the Spanish captain first realised the dire peril he had inadvertently sailed into, his large galleon had been blessed with the bounty of a good head start. Now, hours later, as the Captain stood nervously on the quarter deck of the Juliana, and glanced over his shoulder towards the English frigate for the hundredth time, he could see that despite the best efforts of his frightened and sweating crew, the gap between the two vessels had substantially decreased. Nervously, he wrung his hands and fretted. Very soon he thought; the Juliana would be in range of the Englishman's guns. In an hour, perhaps two at the most, the frigate would draw parallel with his lumbering ship and open fire. Captain Sanchez knew his vessel was blessed with some defensive cannon, but these ruthless English devil ships, which prowled the coastal waters like phantoms, were built to be faster and more manoeuvrable than his own wallowing galleon.

He had never encountered an English privateer before and his knowledge of battle was scant. He would pray to the blessed Madonna and try to disable his enemy with a full broadside. If he failed to bring his own guns to bear, then capture or sinking would, he reflected sadly, be a foregone conclusion.

Like a caged and hungry lion, Sir Richard Starkey, Captain of the Sea Hawk, prowled his own quarter deck, his eyes unwavering and fixed firmly on his fleeing quarry.

Since arriving three weeks earlier, there had been nothing but disappointment; no ships sighted and no spoils to capture off the torturous reef-filled coastline. Now at last, it seemed fortune had smiled. He was close to securing his first prize since leaving Plymouth, so many months earlier. Sir Richard had felt his pulse quicken and more than a little relief, when he sighted the Spaniard and immediately ordered pursuit, to the delight of the crew, as the Sea Hawk's gun ports were hoisted open.

Besides Sir Richard, a man of bird-like stature suddenly dropped his quill, abandoned his map making table and dashed once more to the ship's side rail. Richard smiled to himself. In all his years at sea, he had never known a man to be so violently seasick, in even the gentlest of swells.

Master Humble Godshaw, gentleman mapmaker to the Court of Queen Elizabeth, groaned as his slender frame slumped against the wooden guardrail. His heaving stomach churned once again, as he retched noisily over the side.

'Sea legs escaped you again this morning, Master Godshaw?' Sir Richard shook his head. 'Breakfast not to your liking, I presume?'

Humble Godshaw turned to address his Captain, but the mention of food was too much for his turbulent stomach. His eyes rolled suddenly; his miserable face carried the faintest pallor of green as he spun around and vomited violently again over the side.

Sir Richard caught the eye of his first officer, William Howard, who was also watching the man's distress with poorly concealed amusement. Advice, thought Howard, would probably fall on deaf ears this time, but felt it his duty to give it anyway.

'A good plate of salted herring and a stiff brandy will sort you out, Mister.' He called across the gently rolling deck with a grin. 'Then a stroll around the deck for a few minutes in the fresh sea breeze....Why?' he said, slapping his own stomach, 'Then you'll have your sea legs Mister, and an iron constitution, stronger than mine!'

Wiping specks of fresh vomit from the corners of his gasping mouth, Humble Godshaw, as expected, ignored the first

17

officer's advice. Between groans, in a shaking voice he addressed his Captain.

'Permission to leave the quarter deck, Captain? I'm sorry Sir...I...I need to lie down.'

Sir Richard nodded, unable to stifle a grin any longer. While until now, the Hawk had been unsuccessful in finding a target for her guns, Humble Godshaw had, between regular and explosive bouts of seasickness, produced highly accurate charts, mapping great river deltas, sunken reefs and the twists and turns of the Yucatan Peninsula's sinuous coastline.

'Aye, away with you man. Come back on deck and resume your duties when you feel recovered.'

Nodding his thanks and still clutching his stomach, the mapmaker remained silent as he staggered through the nearest hatchway and disappeared into the gloom inside.

Dismissing the incident as his smile faded, Sir Richard called up to the lookout in the crow's nest high above.

'*Ahoy there!* What can you see? Is the horizon clear?'

The response from above was almost immediate. The lookout cupped his hand to his mouth and shouted down his reply.

'No sign of other ships, Captain, but looks like there's some weather brewing, off to the north.'

Glancing towards the darkening northern horizon, Richard raised his hand in acknowledgement to the pointing lookout; he turned his attention back to his fleeing quarry.

'A shot across her bow first, Will. I want that ship intact, so we'll give them one chance to surrender.'

The First Officer nodded,

'Judging by the number of gun ports, she's probably well-armed, Sir Richard. What if the Spaniard ignores the warning, and won't heave-to?'

Richards's handsome face smiled again, but the smile carried the frigid chill of distant winter. His eyes glared as he shook his head,

'I don't expect them to heave-to, but I have a plan when they run. She's too big, and as you say, probably too well-armed for us to get engaged in a slugging match.' Sir Richard stroked his chin for a moment, and then he said, 'We'll get a little closer yet, and then turn hard over. Give her stern a broadside as our guns come to bear.' Sir Richard's eyes were now as cold as the mirthless smile which still lingered. 'I want her rudder smashed and her mizzen taken down Will. Have our guns loaded with chain shot. She's to be disabled, but not sunk. Once we've crippled her, we'll sweep her decks with a broadside of grape if necessary, then grapple and board her. Is that clear?'

The Sea Hawk's First Officer understood perfectly. Turning his gaze back to the fleeing Spaniard, eyes dancing with anticipation, he said,

'By the way she sits low in the water; she will make a valuable first prize, Captain.'

The Sea Hawk's First Officer grinned hungrily when Sir Richard nodded his agreement. Touching his wide-brimmed hat in acknowledgement, William Howard strode confidently to the forward rail and called down to the cramped deck below, where his gun crews waited patiently to bring the chase to a close. In their midst stood a giant of a man; green eyed and red-haired. It was his deck; apart from his other duties as Sir Richard's manservant, Quinn was fulfilling his role as the Sea Hawk's master gunner.

William Howard cupped his hand to his mouth and shouted down to the giant waiting eagerly for his orders.

'One shot across the Spaniards bows on the Captain's signal, Quinn. If she does not heave-to immediately, we'll come hard over and take her rudder and mizzen as soon as she's in range. The Captain only wants the Spaniard disabled... then we'll board her. A single ball off her bow for the warning, but load the other guns with chainshot. The captain's order is simple. For God's sake, man...don't sink her!'

Quinn remained silent and acknowledged his orders with a brief touch of his huge hand to his forelock. The crews crouching around the ship's 8-pounder cannons looked away from their master gunner and grinned to each other. They were rough and ready, harbour dregs to a man, hired from the shadows of the smoke-filled taverns of Plymouth, where six months previously they had rubbed shoulders in dark corners, exchanging gossip and whispers with smugglers and pirates, as they waited for a ship that would make their fortune from scavenging distant seas. Their eyes glittered, and the crewmen's hearts raced; they smelt valuable prize money, when the fleeing Spaniard was theirs. One heavily tattooed gunner licked his lips, stood up and drew his cutlass. He spat on the flat razor-sharp blade.

'Yeah, we'll have 'em, right enough; that's once we've had our fun with her crew!'

For a moment, crude mutterings and bloodthirsty laughter echoed across the cramped gun deck. Cooped up aboard the Sea Hawk for six tedious months, despite their duties, the seamen had quickly become bored with hard discipline and monotonous daily routine, as they sailed slowly westwards across the empty grey Atlantic. The idea of pricking helpless captives offered welcome distraction. Even greater though, was the thought of their share of rich booty. Both options held great favour, to the harbour scum who manned the Sea Hawk.

'Belay that, Irish Jack!' snarled Quinn, his green eyes blazing. 'The captain will not permit killing of helpless men.'

The master gunner drew himself up to his full imposing height,

'Put up your sword and get back to your position...*NOW!*

Quinn knew their captain better than Irish Jack and the rest of the other fifty-six men aboard the English privateer.

Three years earlier, the giant Cornishman had faithfully served Sir Richard, as his manservant, throughout the terrible siege of Malta, when 40,000 battle-hardened Muslim Turks had landed on the tiny island, intent of annihilating the Catholic Order of the Knights of St John – the last of the Crusaders who defended the strongholds of St. Elmo, St Angelo and St Michael; three great Christian fortresses built by the Order to defend Malta's only two deep-water harbours.

With the destruction of the seafaring Knights who threatened their flank, the Turkish Generals planned to springboard from the tiny island onto mainland Europe's southern shores. When their invasion commenced, the great Muslim host would begin a campaign of conquest and religious conversion, sweeping all before them, and spreading the word of Islam at the point of their swords.

On his Queen's order, Sir Richard had landed on Malta just days before the Turks arrived. To the Knights of St. John, he answered the call to arms made by his uncle Oliver; principal secretary to the Order's Grand master, Jean Parisot La Valette. Although suspected and denounced as a heretic English protestant spy by a small clique of French and Spanish noblemen, with sage advice from his Catholic uncle, a generous serving of good fortune and Quinn's invaluable help, he survived months of swirling intrigue and terrible battle on the tiny island.

When the two men first met, Sir Richard had saved Quinn's life; however, in the ways of war, Quinn had repaid the favour twice over before the great siege was ended. The fighting was bloody and intense. There was merciless slaughter on both sides; Quinn and Sir Richard had been embroiled in countless desperate battles with the invading Turks, but despite La Valette's standing order, to show no mercy to the infidel

21

invaders, Sir Richard had never knowingly dispatched an unarmed enemy.

Quinn knew his master to be a brave and decent English knight; a man of honour, who took his vows to protect the defenceless seriously, but in a cruel twist of fate, something terrible happened during their last days on Malta. Within the Order, the dark shadow of treachery had shrouded his masters grieving soul, when years previously, the great siege was lifted.

Like so many other brave defenders, both master and servant had been sorely wounded during the Turkish invasion, but somewhere during the campaign; a strong bond of loyalty and friendship had grown between them. Their physical wounds had eventually healed, but Quinn knew his master carried one deep and painful hurt, which stubbornly refused to mend. It was a wound beyond the sight of mortal man. There was no healing herb or soothing ointment, for what ailed his master. Sir Richard's brave heart was cruelly broken on the dry and barren island of Malta, with the murder of Miriam, daughter of the Order's Alchemist, Salazar; the woman Richard adored, and planned to marry when they returned to England.

* * *

With a mumbled curse, the tattooed seaman reluctantly slid his cutlass back into its worn leather scabbard. In quieter times, in the hushed corners of the mess deck below, his crew mates knew Irish Jack by another name. The livid red line which marked his face from ear to corner of lifeless mouth had earned him the nickname of Scarface. It was not used openly, lest the culprit received much worse from the point of Irish Jack's dagger. There was no disguising the defiance or menace in the mutilated man's voice as he turned to the crewmen crouched around him.

22

'Then let's see how many are still left alive when we've finished with them, eh lads?'

Quinn ignored the nods and feral grunts of agreement whispered among the crew. Irish Jack was a natural ringleader, and had been an insolent and troublesome thorn in Quinn's side, since the man had made his mark on the ship's articles of war in Plymouth months earlier, but this was not the moment to discipline him. He would deal with Irish Jack's defiance later, in his own way. Quinn had more important things to attend to. He glared and snarled at the scarred crewman standing defiantly before him.

'If I know the Captain, those Spaniards who survive will be spared.' Wiping his hand across his mouth, Quinn snarled again. 'Now get back to your gun, you lazy scum...'

Irish Jack turned and muttered quietly to himself.

'I'll teach you a lesson, you English bastard. I'm going to stick you, first chance I get...'

Chapter Two

Sitting on his beautifully hand-tooled saddle, inlaid with shining silver, the sweating nobleman lent forward and patted his horse's neck. The Spanish Don detested this stinking jungle hellhole. It was far too hot and unbearably humid; very different from the dry heat of civilised and cultured Spain. Only recently torn from the luxury of the Royal Courts of Madrid, Don Rodrigo Salvador Torrez had hungrily assumed his new position; appointed as his majesty's Provincial Governor of Veracruz. The lure of great wealth had beckoned, and Don Rodrigo was not a man to let a literally golden opportunity slip through his fingers.

He was learning, to his growing dismay, that there were abundant irksome duties associated with his new high office. They soured the fortune and power of which he dreamt. As the province's chief administrator, he was also the Magistrate General, which bestowed on him the power of life and death over any who had the misfortune to come before him.

This morning's charade; wasting valuable time having to be in attendance when his sentence was carried out, irked the Don. That was clearly evident from the sour look on the nobleman's pinched face. To add to his annoyance and discomfort, bloodsucking flies constantly buzzed around him and seemed intent on eating him alive. He slapped again at something, which buzzed loudly, close to the back of his neck.

As Don Rodrigo sat uncomfortably in his saddle, behind him, several of his junior staff officers and two priests of the grandly titled Tribunal of the Holy Office of the Inquisition shuffled awkwardly, as they too stood enveloped in the same cloud of buzzing insects. Like those around them, both priests sweated in the oppressive heat. Their duty demanded that they act as the Church's official observers, in the proceedings of the

24

Don's hastily arranged alfresco court. The younger of the hooded priests gently swung an incense burner to and fro, as he mumbled a continuous string of prayers into the aromatic cloud which enveloped both Inquisitors, but did little to dissuade the flies.

A short distance from the Don's entourage, barefoot and barely clothed in torn and filthy rags, a small group of chained slaves stood with heads bowed in sullen silence. They were assembled to witness punishment, then spread word to the other slaves, who toiled night and day in the nearby mines, of the dire consequences of attempted escape. Stern faced guards armed with musket and pike watched them closely, ready to use their weapons on any who showed the slightest sign of unrest or dissent.

After the escapees overpowered the sleeping watch and quickly disappeared into the night, the weakest and most wretched fugitives had been easily tracked, and quickly recaptured. A handful had made good their escape, and vanished into the surrounding jungle, but most had been returned within hours, in chains, to the glade which had been hacked from the virgin jungle, close to the mine's entrance. Don Rodrigo had ordered the trees felled, and their surrounding undergrowth cleared when he first arrived and assumed his duties as regional Governor. Experience had taught him there was always need for a formal place of execution; to instil fear in his captives and make stark example of those caught rebelling against the word of his high office.

The Don had imperiously listened to his obsequious sergeant's report of the previous night's escape, and then immediately made his decision and passed sentence. No appeal for clemency was allowed in Don Rodrigo's court; his word *was* the law. Eyes downcast, the condemned stood side by side, their arms tightly pinioned, beneath the thick wooden cross-member

25

of the scaffold above them. Each of the unfortunate, exhausted escapees balanced precariously on a long narrow plank, which held them several feet clear of the leaf littered ground.

A corpulent Spanish sergeant-at-arms, dressed in breastplate armour and Morion style helmet, stood halfway up a wooden ladder, which rested against the framework of the heavy timber scaffold. He had almost finished placing a rough noose around the last prisoner's neck. With a final jerk of the hemp rope, he was satisfied. The sweating sergeant's lips curled back into a cruel grin, displaying his rotten teeth. Staring into the sweating prisoner's terrified eyes from just inches away, he released the rope. As a parting gesture, he gently patted the man's terrified face. With a leer, he whispered.

'You will dance soon savage....Adios, amigo!'

Seeing all was at last ready, Don Rodrigo turned and snapped at one of the priests.

'Get on with it, man!'

Both monks were dressed in long brown habits, gathered at the waist with worn leather belts. The older and more senior of the two Inquisitors, a qualifier, stepped forward. His face hidden, he clutched his rosary tight to his chest as he prepared himself to do God's work. Clearing his throat, he regarded the condemned slaves from within the dark shadow of his cowl. He began to speak as if he was giving them a last sermon, which in fact, he was. To the backdrop of noisy cries from exotic birds hidden in the lush surrounding jungle, the priest's voice rang throughout the stifling atmosphere of the hot and fetid clearing.

'We are gathered here today, in the sight of almighty God...'

The Catholic Church was a powerful influence in the New World. Its support was vital to Don Rodrigo's plan to extract his fortune from the mines surrounding Veracruz. Allowing the

26

attendant priests any opportunity to gain converts would stand him in good stead with his Grace, Bishop Acosta. Even these miserable wretches about to die were acceptable converts. Don Rodrigo realised there could be trouble if he ignored the Church's influence. If he so wished, the Bishop could send sealed dispatches, and complain directly to his majesty the King, or even worse, to the Pontiff in Rome, concerning Don Rodrigo's excessive and cruel treatment of his slaves. There were Church protocols concerning their handling, which since his arrival, in order to increase production, Don Rodrigo had deliberately ignored.

Being recalled to Madrid to answer charges in the ecclesiastical courts would incur a year's round trip, and the Don trusted nobody to handle his affairs while he was gone. He had no intention of wasting a minute longer than was absolutely necessary to lift the punitive mortgage on his family's future, in this foul, God-forsaken land.

Conversion or redemption of heathen souls worked together with the Church's avaricious grab for their own share of the New World's riches, and Bishop Acosta was no fool. Despite being publicly sworn to a life of poverty and chastity, both souls and gold held equal merit in the eyes of the Bishop. However, as far as Don Rodrigo was concerned, every moment of his time was precious. He allowed this charade to proceed purely to gain favour in the Bishop's eyes; the priests of the Inquisition had gone through the motions of redemption and failed miserably, so now it was time to act. A stark lesson demonstrating the penalty of escape must be made, and the terrified captives provided the perfect opportunity for Don Rodrigo's point to be made.

* * *

'The penalty for attempting to escape is death!'

The old priest's voice reached every ear in the clearing,

'Your fair trial is complete and legal sentence has been pronounced by the Governor, his Excellency Don Rodrigo Salvador Torrez.' The priest inclined his head respectfully towards the Governor before returning his attention to the swaying prisoners standing beneath the scaffold.

'Shortly you will die...' His words floated away on the clearing's humid air. 'But in its boundless mercy, Holy Mother Church gives you one last chance to salvage your eternal souls. Take the Holy sacrament and convert now from your Godless pagan ways to Christianity. As good Christians, your sins will be forgiven, and your cleansed souls will fly straight to Heaven.' The white-haired priest's face changed. Beneath the course shade of his cowl, his wrinkled face suddenly hardened as he issued his dire warning. 'The eternal fires of Hell await those of you who refuse this last chance of redemption...to the one true faith.'

The older priest turned and nodded to a slave who had been separated from the prisoners brought from the mine as witnesses. Sternly he said.

'Translate the words of God, my son.'

The slave nodded and spoke rapidly in his native Mayan tongue. The captives balanced on the wooden bar listened carefully, then looked at each other. One old man stood in their midst, frail and wizened. He shouted something back to the translator.

'Well, what did he say?' snapped the priest, when the old man fell silent.

The translator quickly replied. 'He is a Shaman holiness; a village healer who speaks to the spirits of the dead on behalf of his people. He asks; do the iron-shirts also go to this place called Heaven, when they die?'

Surprised and irritated, the white-haired cleric snapped. 'Well...Yes, of course they do!'

28

The condemned Shaman listened to the translator's short reply. He thought for a moment and then shook his head. He whispered something to the condemned prisoners beside him. Some momentarily forgot their terror and grinned broadly as the Shaman turned his attention back to the Spanish priest. To the assembled Spaniard's surprise, the old man threw back his head and laughed. His expression and shouted answer put fear into the translator.

With hooded eyes the senior priest of the Inquisition pierced his interpreter with a cold and baleful stare. He snapped at the man.

'Well?'

'Ah...Holiness. The...the Shaman says to live life eternal beside the iron-shirts in your place called Heaven *would* be Hell for him...and all his people.'

Without waiting for the priest's reply, the Shaman called out again, but this time the old man's eyes narrowed to slits. Staring straight at Don Rodrigo, he snarled something else in his native tongue.

In shock, the translator stepped back, shaking his head as the old man's last words faded. Whatever the Shaman had said, it put genuine terror in the man's dark native eyes.

The grinning witchdoctor defiantly hawked and spat on the ground, to reinforce his contempt for the white men's shallow offer of life eternal. The prisoners bound on either side of him did the same.

Don Rodrigo sat waiting to hear the translation of the Shaman's last words. More for the benefit of the attendant priests than his own interest, he snapped at the cowering translator.

'I haven't got all day, man...What did he say, damn you?'

'Ah...Excellency'...The native translator avoided eye contact and kept his head bowed low. 'The Shaman has called down a

29

curse on you. He said evil befalls evil and soon the jungle's Gods will send you on your way to ruin!'

With a muffled curse, Don Rodrigo's eyes narrowed at the holy man's defiance. He wrenched his bridle hard over. Turning his head sharply backwards, first to the priests, and then the fat sergeant, he snarled.

'Damn their insolence. Their souls cannot be saved. Carry out the sentence. *Hang them all...NOW!'*

Chapter Three

'Remember Quinn, I want her stopped...Not sent to the bottom.'

Standing behind the gun mounted forward on the Sea Hawk's port side, Quinn grinned up at his Captain.

'Aye Master, I understand!'

With the grin still playing across his craggy sun-burnt face, Quinn turned his gaze away from his master and the crowded quarterdeck, towards the fat stern of the fleeing galleon. The shot would take great care, as the swell was becoming heavier. He must place the 8lb cannonball as close to the front of the other ship's bow as was humanly possible. When the gun roared, the Sea Hawk's deadly message to stop must be sudden, plain and absolute.

To confirm the lookout's earlier report, a squall had appeared on the northern horizon during the last hours of the pursuit, coming closer as Sir Richard had remorselessly narrowed the gap with the fleeing Spaniard. Banks of dark rain-laden clouds scudded across the blue skies towards them, as both ships rocked and ploughed through the increasing swell. Adjusting his balance on the rolling bow deck, Quinn crouched down behind the cannon's fat barrel as he waited patiently for its muzzle to clear the enemy's beam, giving him the perfect moment to fire. He absently tapped a rhythm on the cannon's cold barrel, as he watched his fleeing target.

The Spaniard's stern was clearly visible as the Sea Hawk plunged onwards, sailing ever closer to its quarry. Sir Richard had ordered his top-men to add extra sail; now it was paying dividends as the Sea Hawk quickly played out its last deadly dance with the Santa Juliana.

Quinn looked at the five members of the gun crew who were crouched around their cannon.

31

'Stand by to reload with chain shot when we fire.' He shook his head grimly. 'I know the Captain, there won't be two warnings. If the Spaniard don't stop immediately, the captain wants her crippled.'

The seamen nodded eagerly. Like the rest of the crewmen manning the Hawk's guns, they knew exactly what to do. Two cannon balls linked by a short length of stout chain would cleave the mast of any ship, but the double shot was unlikely to penetrate the Spaniard's thick oak-clad hull. One of the gunners lifted the heavy double-balled shot from an ammunition locker and rested it alongside the cannon. The rest of the Sea Hawk's guns were already loaded with the deadly shot. Eager anticipation of the battle to come was written all over the gun crews scarred and sweating faces.

Sir Richard was standing close behind, watching the last stage of the chase unfold before him.

He nodded down towards his manservant.

'Fire when your gun bears, Quinn.'

The Sea Hawk ploughed on through the white tipped waters as Quinn waited patiently for the moment when his forward gun would bear just beyond the prow of the fleeing ship. Carefully watching the enemy bow, and the rise and fall of the gun's muzzle, he suddenly stepped to one side and turned to the crewman holding the lighted match secured to a long wooden rod.

Quinn's eyes glittered as he took one last look and gave the order. Now was his moment.

'Fire!'

The gunner leaned forward and stabbed his smoking fuse into the primed touch hole of the waiting eight-pounder. The fine black powder ignited instantly with a bright flash and puff of smoke. A heartbeat later, with a thunderous roar the cannon bucked and recoiled in a cloud of black acrid smoke. At incredible speed the heavy iron cannonball flew above the white

32

tipped waves past the galleon's hull. With a mighty splash, the ball impacted less than 50 feet in front of the Spanish merchantman. The white tower of frothing water sent a clear and unequivocal message to both its Spanish captain and his crew.

Within seconds, the master of the Santa Juliana knew he would be embroiled in a battle for his life if he did not surrender quickly. Fearfully eyeing the cold churning waters which surrounded his ship, he mopped his brow with a finely embroidered lace handkerchief. He had run out of time, and options. What must he do to save himself, his ship and his crew? The horizon was clear; there was no hope of Spanish men-of-war coming to his aid. Surrender was unthinkable, but so was resistance. With a growing knot of fear in his stomach, he reflected that the English pirates might just as soon slaughter them all if he surrendered. The Santa Juliana's crew stared up towards their captain, their faces filled with terror. He wrung his hands, lost in the agonising turmoil of indecision which engulfed him. What in the name of the blessed Virgin, was he to do?

Sir Richard called down to his master gunner. 'Well done Quinn, any closer you would have sunk her.' Richard turned back to his first officer. 'Prepare the grappling irons and make sure the men are fully prepared for boarding, when I give the order.'

Suddenly, a puff of smoke and echoing boom erupted from the Spaniard's stern gun, followed immediately by a whoosh and spray of seawater, as its cannonball struck the foaming bow of the Sea Hawk, just below the waterline. The English privateer bucked and shuddered through its length and breadth with the sudden crashing impact.

Almost in disbelief, Richard's First Officer shouted,

'They're making a fight of it, Captain!'

The Juliana was now lying just a few hundred yards ahead of the Hawk. Richard turned his head to the steersman who held the Sea Hawk's great wheel tightly in his broad calloused hands. The English knight's eyes never left the fleeing Spanish ship as he raised his arm,

'Get ready to turn hard to larboard on my signal...wait...wait,' keeping his arm raised, Richard looked at his first officer and then spoke calmly to him. 'Give the Spaniard's stern a full rolling broadside as your guns bear, if you please Will.'

Lieutenant Howard nodded.

'Aye Sir, I know what to do,' he ran quickly to the rail.

'Port gun crews...Stand by… Fire as your guns bear.'

Richard suddenly dropped his arm.

'*NOW!* Steersman. Hard 'a larboard!'

The crewman began to swing the heavy wheel. The nimble Sea Hawk answered the helm immediately, yawing steeply over, some ninety degrees away from its original line of pursuit. Quinn was watching intently through the open port of his No. 1 gun. The high stern of the Spanish galleon hove majestically into view.

'Rolling broadside, fire as your guns bear, lads!.... *FIRE!*'

With a thunderous roar, Number 1 gun fired. With a whirring hiss, the chain shot flew over the churning waters towards the Spaniard's stern. The impact was catastrophic to the thick oaken blade of the ship's tall rudder. Its midsection disintegrated suddenly into a hissing cloud of razor-sharp wooden splinters, which splashed into the rolling waters behind the wounded ship. Seconds later, the second of Sea Hawk's portside battery fired, adding to the destruction aboard the shuddering galleon. Repeatedly, the English guns crashed in great clouds of fire and smoke. The fifth shot took the Spaniard's mizzen mast. Like a great tree cut down in the forest, the mast creaked and groaned as it slowly toppled over, carrying

34

rigging, shredded sails and several unlucky Spanish sailors with it. The shattered mast splashed overboard into the waiting waters, which swirled and foamed around the Juliana's wooden hull.

A resounding cheer went up from the crew of the Sea Hawk, as the helpless merchantman's answer to the dramatic broadside appeared before them, just seconds later. Knowing his position was hopeless, unable to steer or make further headway; her Spanish master decided honour was satisfied. Having at least offered token resistance, he ordered the galleon's colours struck, sending the universally recognised signal of surrender to the English ship, now lying less than two hundred yards off his starboard beam. The Imperial banner of Spain was quickly lowered from the flagstaff, which adorned what was left of her battered wooden stern. Men could be clearly seen frantically climbing into her remaining rigging, to take in her billowing sails.

Sir Richard turned his gaze from the seamen aboard the stricken ship. He looked away for a moment towards the darkening rain-filled clouds closing fast from the north.

'Cease-fire and bring the Hawk alongside the Spaniard, as quickly as you can, William. I want her grappled and boarded well before the squall hits us,' with a knowing nod he said. 'Add the starboard gunners to the boarding party. Keep the port gun crews at their stations until we have our prize secured.' Sir Richard grinned wolfishly and raised an eyebrow, 'just in case the Spaniards forget they have surrendered.'

* * *

As the remaining sullen slaves were herded back to the mine, Don Rodrigo called to their sergeant. He pointed at the limp forms of the executed prisoners, who swayed gently beneath the gibbet's crossbar.

'Cut down the bodies, but leave their witchdoctor where he hangs, until his body rots. That should remind all these lazy scum who is master here, and what their reward will be if they dare attempt another escape.'

The fat sergeant bowed respectfully. In this fetid heat, the stink from the corpse would soon become appalling; his nose wrinkled absently at the thought. But it was not a sergeant's place to bring this to the Governors attention, so keeping his head bowed, he muttered.

'Si, your Excellence, I shall see to it immediately. '

With a curt nod, Don Rodrigo pulled his bridle hard around and kicked his spurs into his horse's flanks. As the sun continued to rise in the blue heavens, followed by his lieutenants and priests, he began the long ride back to Veracruz.

* * *

There had been something in the way the shrivelled little man's eyes had glittered, which troubled the Spanish nobleman. Despite the heat, he shivered involuntarily as he thought of the Shaman's bitter hatred as he spoke his final words. For just a moment, something dark and terrible had washed over Don Rodrigo's soul before the man had swung. Silently cursing his own superstitious foolishness, Don Rodrigo shrugged off more thought of the old man, or the empty curse, laid upon the Don's soul. More earthly matters demanded he sought the cool shade of his Governor's palace; the morning would soon be gone, and to his dismay, the day seemed intent on growing hotter by the minute.

* * *

Thrown by the strongest of the privateer's crewmen, a dozen grappling hooks snaked across the narrow gap between

36

the two ships. They clanked loudly against the wooden rails which protected the Spaniard's main deck, as English barb's bit deep into the Spaniard's salt-stained timbers. Another barrage of barbed iron crossed the lapping water below, and a tangled lattice of ropes quickly secured the Sea Hawk and the crippled Santa Juliana together.

Quinn punched the air in triumph. Cupping his hands to his mouth, he barked at the waiting boarding party.

'Well done lads...Now the rest of you...grab them ropes, *and heave!*

Sir Richard watched as small knots of his heavily armed crewmen scurried across the main deck, grabbing at the flaccid ropes. Quickly taking up the slack, they began pulling them taut. Quinn stood behind the lines of straining crewmen, shouting a mixture of praise and curses, loudly encouraging them as they took the strain and heaved the two ships close enough for the boarding party to scramble across the narrowing gap and board their prize. Since the deadly broadside, the Sea Hawk's guns had remained silent, but Sir Richard was taking no chances. The port gun crews remained crouched at their posts behind loaded guns and open ports, while eight of his crewmen stood along the decks of the Sea Hawk, their matchlocks levelled at the sullen Spanish sailors standing with their hands raised; impotent and helpless, aboard the crippled merchant galleon.

With a combined final heave by the freely sweating seamen, the tug of war ended as the two ships bumped together. Sir Richard cupped his hand to his mouth at the grinding impact. He gave the order his crew had been eagerly waiting for.

'Board!'

With blood-curdling battle cries, the Sea Hawk's boarding party sprang onto the ships narrow guard rail waving cutlasses and axes in their tattooed hands. Steadying themselves with the grapple lines, they leapt onto the Juliana's gently rolling deck.

37

Within moments, Sir Richard had left his quarterdeck. Calling over his shoulder for Quinn to follow him, Richard joined his men aboard the Spanish vessel. At a nod from their Captain, the English crew fanned out around the merchantman's decks; her terrified crew were quickly rounded up and herded at sword and gunpoint towards the stern of the crippled Spanish ship.

'Some of you get below, lads; search out any stragglers and bring them up on deck.' Sir Richard looked up towards the group of surrendered officers on the Spaniard's quarterdeck, who stood silently awaiting their fate,

'Quinn... take two men and bring their Captain to me.'

With a chorus of 'Aye, Captain' some of the Sea Hawk's men remained with levelled muskets to guard the newly captured crew while the remainder of the boarding party split into twos and threes. Disappearing through hatches and open doorways they begin rummaging below decks for anyone who might be hiding. Quinn nodded and lumbered up the ladder which connected the two decks. With his scimitar clutched in his huge hand he pointed it's wickedly curved blade towards the knot of officers who were huddled beside the Santa Juliana's wheel. The shining Ottoman blade was a prize given to him by his master during their adventures on Malta; it was Quinn's most treasured possession.

'Which one of you is Capitano?' He growled menacingly. The colour drained from several Spanish officers faces as the giant English pirate towered over them. Nervously, their Captain stepped forward. After years of trading in English waters, Captain Hernando Sanchez understood. His ship was taken; he had nothing left to retaliate with but his anger.

'I am Captain,' he spluttered haughtily. 'I must protest. This is outrageous act of piracy against Spain.'

Quinn grinned at the man's words. He remained silent and with a jerk of his head motioned the Juliana's master towards the

38

ladder. Quinn leered and swept his empty hand towards the gun deck, where Sir Richard stood waiting.

'Save it for my Captain... He wants to talk to you.'

With a resigned nod, Captain Sanchez stepped away from his officers and shuffled in the direction Quinn indicated.

Chapter Four

Sir Richard stared at his vanquished enemy for several moments before he spoke.

'You may keep your sword, Captain.'

The master of the captured galleon bowed slightly. In heavily accented English, he replied, 'I am most grateful, Senor.' Straightening his embroidered and ornate jacket, the Spaniard looked his captor in the eye.

'I am Captain Hernando Sanchez, Master of the Santa Juliana, and I protest at this gross act of piracy most strongly... You have absolutely no right to attack a ship of his majesty's trading fleet in this fashion. We were about our lawful business...And as far as I am aware Senor, our two counties are not at war.'

Sir Richard forced back a smile. He looked about at the debris of shattered timbers surrounding the devastated mast, and the untidy gaggle of captives herded onto the equally devastated stern of his newly acquired prize. He raised an eyebrow to acknowledge both the introduction, and the questions.

'I am Sir Richard Starkey, Master of the Sea Hawk. I believe my guns give me all the right I need, Senor.' He shrugged. 'And war between England and Spain is surely only a matter of time...is it not?

Refusing to answer the question, Captain Sanchez ground his teeth in frustration before he changed tack and asked,

'What is to become of my crew, Captain? You are pirates are you not?' Will you kill us all?'

Sir Richard stroked his chin as he contemplated the Spaniard's fate. Turning away from his prisoner for a moment, he winked at Quinn. Turning back to face Sanchez, he thought for a moment longer, and then, stern faced, he replied.

'Yes, it is a most serious question, Captain. If you are correct in your assumption that I command a common pirate ship, why, I suppose I should order my men to butcher you and your crew where they stand, and throw what's left overboard?'

In an instant, the master of the Juliana stepped back in horror. He opened his mouth to protest while his eyes flicked nervously at several grinning members of the boarding party who were standing close by, guns levelled. One had burning eyes, and a livid scar running across his jaw.

The man drew a dagger from his belt. The coals within his eyes glittered as they bored into the captured Spaniard,

'Just give us the order, Captain...'

Sir Richard held up his hand to stop Irish Jack from his murderous intent,

'No!'

Turning his attention back to Sanchez, he said.

'I am certainly an English Privateer Captain, but the Sea Hawk is no pirate ship. The distinction may be a narrow one, but it has saved your life and the lives of your crew today. I don't hold with killing helpless men. I will not stain my hands, or my family's honour with the blood of unarmed prisoners.' Sir Richard turned to his first officer. 'See to it that our prisoners are put ashore as soon as possible, William.' Sir Richard turned back to Captain Sanchez, 'When you land, follow the coastline due north towards your nearest settlement. My charts indicate that there is one less than twenty miles away. I will allow you sufficient water for your wounded, but no weapons other than your sword. If you set off at first light tomorrow, you should reach safety before nightfall.

Captain Sanchez nodded with relief. He had heard stories of the savage English and their habit of throwing captured crews overboard, to take their chances with the hungry sharks and barracuda which patrolled these waters. He silently thanked the

41

blessed Madonna. He knew he was extremely lucky to stand before a merciful captor.

'On behalf of my officers and crew, I am most grateful to you, Sir Richard. I will inform the Governor of your mercy, when we reach Boca Del Rio.

Richard nodded gravely. His mercy came at a price.

'Very well, Captain. I request you remind your men that they are my prisoners, and survival depends on their good behaviour, until they are released ashore. If just one of them tries anything...' Sir Richard nodded towards the churning seas beyond the rail. The Spaniards eyes flicked nervously beyond the ship's rail. There was no need for more between them; the unspoken threat was eloquent enough. As the Spaniard turned to re-join his officers, Sir Richard held out his hand and added.

'Ah yes, Captain, there is one more thing. The keys to your strong room, if you please…'

With a sigh, Captain Sanchez stopped and reached inside his shirt. The iron key was attached to a thin chain, which for added security; he habitually wore around his neck. He reluctantly removed it and handed it to Richard's First Officer.

'Go below, and report back to me when you have made an inventory of what the Juliana has in her hold.'

With a triumphant grin, William nodded. With a slight bow, he said. 'It will be my pleasure, Sir.'

As the grumbling prisoners were herded down to their quarters and put under close guard, Sir Richard set about ordering temporary repairs to the Juliana's devastated rudder. With one eye on the approaching storm, time was of the essence. If their valuable prize was caught, unable to steer in heavy seas, there could be but one outcome; the ship would flounder and be lost. He ordered his ships carpenters to assess the damage, and make such repairs as they could. Engrossed in solving the problems he now faced, he failed to notice Quinn's arrival. The giant Cornishman's face betrayed something serious as he cleared his throat. Tugging on his forelock, Quinn said,

'Begging pardon, master. Message has just come over from the Hawk... The Spaniards only shot did more damage than we've realised.'

Richard whirled around and faced his manservant.

What? he snapped.

'Err...It's put a hole in the old girl's bow, just below the waterline. The Hawk's taking on water real fast, Sir...The message said... she's sinking!'

* * *

The Governor of Veracruz slammed his fist hard onto the table. His anger at the Juliana's apparent loss was clearly evident to the assembled naval captains, who stood nervously before him.

'Well get back out to sea and find them, damn you! There's always a chance that the Juliana ran aground somewhere along the shoreline during the storm. The cargo must be found and salvaged at all costs if the ship still survives, is that clear?' The Don's voice was shrill, when through clenched teeth he angrily ordered them out of his office.

Don Rodrigo silently cursed the New World in general as he watched the small group of captains make their hasty exit. The beautifully panelled double doors closed with a loud click behind the last of them. He was suddenly alone, cocooned in the quiet which now surrounded him. It was cool in the great marbled office within the Governor's palace, but nevertheless, his blood felt as if it was about to boil. It seemed that everything that could go wrong in this cursed land, invariably did. His mind flicked back momentarily to the shaman's curse. Irritated at his own foolish superstition, Don Rodrigo clawed his mind back to reality.

43

Labour shortages and the native's constant unrest, the unrelenting, oppressive heat and humidity, a myriad of stinging insects and unending interference from that damned Bishop's priests were just some of the problems he faced. Don Rodrigo's days seemed to be filled with nothing but setbacks and bad news. To add to his woes, the Commodore of the flotilla arrived from the north had just reported the disappearance of the Santa Julian in a violent storm.

Don Rodrigo scowled. How on earth, he wondered, was he to make a success of this venture, repay the moneylenders and turn a healthy profit, when he was surrounded by incompetent fools who seemed incapable of sailing even a few miles along the coast without losing ships, and the most precious of cargos?

The fleet was almost fully assembled, and the great mule-train from Peru was due to arrive at the end of the month. The loss of the Juliana's cargo from his northern mines would be a considerable financial loss to Don Rodrigo personally.

When he bought the franchise of the Veracruz Governorship from the King, there had been no mention of facing such reversals during his time in office. Don Rodrigo invested most of his considerable family fortune from his province in the south of Spain, into this expensive enterprise. He even had to borrow heavily from the damned Jews, by mortgaging his own ancestral lands and home to raise the balance of the huge sum the King demanded. Losses now, whatever their cause surely meant a dangerous and uncertain future and smaller profits when the convoy eventually reached the safety of Spain.

Don Rodrigo brooded silently as he sat alone in his office. Since his abrupt return from Malta, and the carnage of its terrible siege by the Turks, it seemed good luck had eluded him. That damned old fool, the Order's Grand master La Valette had virtually thrown him off the island, shortly after the powerful

44

Christian relief column had finally lifted the siege. Many of the surviving Knights of the Order of St John had returned to Spain as heroes, but Don Rodrigo harboured the belief that the Order's ageing leader suspected him of treachery. No proof was ever found of course, the Don was too cunning for that; he had covered his tracks when dealing with the invading Turks too well, but unlike many noblemen that had survived five months of merciless slaughter, no letter of commendation, extolling his valiant bravery had been sent from the Grand Master, to King Phillip in Madrid.

The Don snorted to himself. Damn La Valette, and his English secretary, Oliver Starkey. Despite their quiet investigations immediately after the siege had ended, neither had unearthed any solid proof of his connivance with the Turks; his freedom to return to Spain proved they had been left filled only with unproven suspicions. And damn that heretic Englishman Richard Starkey, the Don thought angrily, who had thwarted his plan to save his own skin by helping the invaders when Christian victory seemed impossible. The Englishman was clearly on Malta as a spy of his heretic Queen, but the old fool who sat upon the Order's throne had constantly refused to accept Don Rodrigo's accusations and believe it not so.

A cruel smile crept onto the Rodrigo's thin face as he remembered. At the time, his accusations had been deflected, but his aim had been true when he ambushed and killed the Englishman's Greek whore, in the confusion of the last great battle, against the remnants of the once proud Ottoman army. In a swirl of smoke and dust, battle raged after the great mine had detonated beneath the fortress walls of St Angelo. Amidst the bloodletting and carnage which ensued; revenge was proven, once again, to be a dish best served cold. He had at least salvaged some small revenge against the heretic English knight, by killing the woman he loved. Only bad fortune had stopped him from finishing Starkey as well, when Don Rodrigo had

45

subsequently gloated over the wounded and helpless Englishman, as the fighting drew to an end.

Casting further melancholy aside, Don Rodrigo refocused his attention to the present. The three ships which had safely arrived from the north were loaded with livestock and provisions for his first convoy's six-month passage to Spain. Their arrival was a relief of course; as without holds filled with foodstuffs and animals, plundered from his northern territories, the crews of the other sixteen ships in the great convoy were doomed to starvation long before they reached the safety of Spain. To the Don's great regret however, the sum total of all the refined bars of precious silver ore mined and smelted over the last six months had been loaded aboard the Juliana, which he now feared had been lost to the sea.

Don Rodrigo cast the quill he had held tightly onto the papers spread across the table before him. At least, the majority of his coming fortune remained safe. The great mule-train from Peru was getting closer every day, bringing the promise of fabulous wealth and huge profit to the House of Torrez. The daily interest the Jews had demanded was both punitive and crippling, but there was no way to rush the opportunity to make repayment. To date, no ship of discovery had yet successfully navigated the roaring waters of the treacherous route around the Continent's southern tip. Without a safe and prudent course from the other side of the New World, the only practical way to transport the immense fortune, dug from the mines of distant Peru, was to carry the freshly smelted bars of gold and silver by mule, almost one hundred leagues through the steaming jungles and across high mountain ranges. He did not envy the men charged with seeing the mule-train safely across such vast distances, but the soldiers involved were sufficiently well-armed to protect the fortune from marauding native tribes, as the great mule-train slowly crossed each of their jungle territories in turn.

46

Don Rodrigo pushed his chair back and stood up. Walking over to a side table, he helped himself to a glass of wine. True, he thought to himself as he brought the crystal goblet to his lips, men were lost all along the ancient trail, to the whispering death of poisoned arrows and silent blowpipe darts, which would kill his men in the span of a few heartbeats. Disease in this pestilent land was an equally efficient killer, but Rodrigo Torrez absently shrugged to himself. He considered the loss of life, by whatever means, to be more than acceptable, as long as the mule-train arrived safely, and intact. The dead required no wages, so their occasional demise would only add to his own profits, when the mule-train finally arrived at what was an oasis of civilisation within the savage and untamed jungles of Mexico; the glittering city of Veracruz.

The Don sniffed absently. If nothing else went wrong, he mused, all would be well, but to replace his losses he urgently needed more manpower to work in the mines. The equation was a simple one; the more who worked by day or night, the more ore would be mined. Slaves were the Don's key to success. With sufficient natives and criminals, forced into hard labour, Torrez was confident he could exceed his quotas, and return home in just a few years as one of the richest men in Spain. Licking his lips with anticipation, he turned his attention to the maps spread across the table. He pondered them for a moment, and then looked up sharply. He called to his secretary, work worked in the adjoining office.

'Fernandez!'

Moments later, there was a soft rap on his door. An older man entered and bowed.

'Yes, Excellency?'

'Order Colonel Alveraz to report to me...*immediately!'*

47

Chapter Five

By the dim light of the swaying lanterns, Sir Richard crouched down in the cramped doorway of the forward cable tier. Quinn stood bent almost double behind him. Both men looked down with growing dismay at the hastily assembled repair party, who stood shivering, waist-deep in a swirl of cold foaming water. Floating debris bobbed around them within the tight confines of the storage space, which lay just below the waterline, inside the ship's wooden hull.

Working in the narrow confines of the claustrophobic semi-darkness, cold and soaked by the turgid water, several men were frantically hammering a fat wooden wedge into the jagged hole left by the Spaniard's only defiant shot. Against the roaring hiss of incoming water, the men's desperate shouts to each another echoed in the small chamber. Suddenly, without warning, with a splintering crash, one of the main spars which held the curved shape of the bow cracked and began to split. If it broke away, there was an immediate and catastrophic danger that the entire spa would be torn from the ship's planking, opening the Hawk's hull to the remorseless inrush of an unforgiving ocean. When they heard the ominous crack, the four men had jumped backwards in sheer terror. More water began to pour into the already half-full tier. The powerful spray instantly extinguished two of the flickering lanterns, adding darkness to the men's terror and confusion.

Realising the terrible danger they were suddenly in, without hesitation, Richard leapt through the narrow doorway and jumped into the roaring rush of swirling water, closely followed by the massive bulk of Quinn. Fighting against the powerful flow and shouldering his terrified crewmen aside, Richard spat out a mouthful of seawater and grabbed at a floating plank.

'Help me jam this against the spa to hold it in position, before it breaks completely, man!'

Quinn's huge hands closed round the other end of the plank and sloshing through the rising water, with his manservant's help, Richard rammed it home and braced it firmly against the damaged spa.

'Put your back against it, and hold it there while I find another plank!' Richard yelled desperately. He frantically cast about in the foaming water for something else to brace the hasty repair. Despite the roaring water which threatened to overwhelm them both at any second, Quinn slammed his powerful shoulder against the plank and straining with every ounce of his enormous strength, held it firmly in position.

Richard found another length of timber and jammed it hard against the other side of the fractured spa. Two of his crewmen had recovered sufficiently to wade through the swirling water and come to their aid.

'Find more spars men. We must strengthen the braces… or we're doomed!'

Numbed by the cold, as the water level continued to rise, the shivering crewmen's efforts were finally rewarded, when the powerful flow of water was suddenly slowed to a thin spray, after Quinn's final whack with a heavy iron-headed hammer to the tight-fitting wooden plug. The ship's forward planking was split and splintered around the freshly bunged hole, but for now at least, the waters inrush was almost stopped by the fat bung, and the hasty braces which supported the damaged main spa beside it.

Quinn turned his attention to another wooden wedge jammed against one of the supports. Water dripped from his shaggy mane of red hair as he growled hopefully,

'Should hold for while then, master?'

With obvious relief in his eyes, Sir Richard nodded.

49

'Aye Quinn, it should do for now, but we must get the water out. The Hawk's sitting heavy by the bow. If we don't get rid of the extra weight quickly, the ship will tip forward and we'll lose steerage.'

With the squall fast approaching, there was only one thing to do, and both men knew it.

'Grab every available man you can find, and form a bucket-chain to the deck.' Richard stared at his servant. 'We must rebalance the ship quickly and get the tier dry. If the squall catches us bow heavy, we're in grave danger of losing both ships.'

Quinn nodded. 'Yes Master, I'll see to it right away.' He turned and lumbered away into the gloomy darkness of the companionway. Richard returned his attention to the chaos inside the cable tier. He reached forward and pulled each of the shivering repair party out of the cold swirling water.

'Well done lads. Now search out anything you can use to get this damned water overboard. Buckets, pans...anything will do. Quinn will be back with help soon, but I need you to start straight away.'

Still in shock and shaking from remembered terror and the frigid chill, each of the shivering crewmen nodded. A chorus of 'Aye captain,' confirmed their understanding; their faces grim, they knew their lives depended on the task ahead.

Richard found his first officer aboard the Juliana.

'William, I have made temporary repair to the Hawk. How soon before we can steer the Spaniard?'

'It will be a while yet, Sir Richard. I've had a man over the stern, who reported the hull is sound, but almost the entire rudder is gone. Our master carpenter says what's left cannot be repaired, it must be replaced completely.' He shook his head. 'But not out here with a storm coming. He says the ship must be beached to effect the rudder's replacement.'

50

It was more bad news but having seen the damage done when his cannon opened fire, Richard had expected nothing less. He cursed softly, then nodded grimly,

'Very well. Chop away what's left of the mizzen and put it over the side quickly. When we can get sufficient water out of the Hawk, we'll take the Spaniard in tow and find somewhere to beach both ships while repairs are made. Search out anything that will hold water William, and then take as many Spanish prisoners as you need over to the Hawk.' Richard turned towards the approaching storm, 'I want at least two bucket chains working as quickly as possible...Clear?'

William Howard nodded vigorously. 'Yes Sir, perfectly clear.'

As the first officer turned to carry out his orders, Richard stopped him abruptly.

'One more thing, Will... Search out Master Godshaw, and send him to my cabin aboard the Hawk with his latest charts....*at once!*'

* * *

Having made his latest inspection of the gold mines to the south, the long ride back to the palace was hot and uneventful. It did nothing to improve the Governor's dark mood. Followed in single file by his usual entourage of nobles, soldiers and priests, Don Rodrigo had walked his horse in silence along the jungle lined track, as his mind returned to the recent execution, as he brooded over the Shaman and his dying curse. Although not a superstitious man by nature, the Governor of Veracruz had been deeply unsettled by something he saw in the witchdoctor's eyes before he died. It was a look that went beyond mere hatred. It was dark and sinister, almost feral. Given the untamed wilderness the Shaman lived in, Don Rodrigo decided it must have reflected the wild animal in the old man. Anyway he thought, there were more pressing issues to be arranged when he arrived back at the palace.

Don Rodrigo had issued a flurry of orders that more patrols were to be sent out into the jungles which hugged the coastline, in search of native fishing settlements. The ocean was bountiful; a limitless source of food for the taking by the natives who lived there, who had so far eluded the Spaniards.

Satisfied that dwindling manpower would quickly be replaced, Don Rodrigo turned to a more pressing matter, on the path to his golden future. He and Colonel Alveraz were locked in conversation.

'But surely we have an agreement with the Mayans Excellency? I thought they were to deliver the last of the ransom in gold you demanded of them next week, on the holy day of the festival of St. Teresa, and you would release their King during the festivities?' Colonel Alveraz sounded shaken. He was caught off guard by this sudden change of plan by the Governor.

A month earlier, Don Rodrigo had ordered him to lead a heavily armed punitive raid against the local Mayan King's inland capital, in retribution for repeated attacks on isolated Spanish outposts. When the relief column of soldiers reached what was left of their comrade's jungle outpost, the musketeers found no survivors. The tough Spanish soldiers were ashen faced and stunned at what they saw when they discovered the grisly fate of their brothers. What they found sickened even the most battle-hardened Conquistadors. Those unfortunate Spaniards who had been taken alive during the Mayan raid had been ritualistically slaughtered. Tied to a makeshift altar, one by one, hearts had been torn from the captive's living bodies; the cruel Mayan's Gods demanded blood to appease them, and the Mayan King's Shaman priests ensured the sacrifices were dedicated to those

52

deities most likely to support the King, in his future battles against the hated invaders.

Spanish muskets easily cut down any man who raised a jade axe or spear against the iron-shirts, when the reprisal within the Mayan principality's capital began. Captured women and children were quickly rounded up, manacled and enslaved. After looting the great Temple pyramid, and his sprawling stone palace, the Mayan King Yikin Calakmul, was taken alive by Alveraz and his Spanish troopers. The Emperor's bodyguard died bravely in a hail of musket fire trying to protect him, but under the Colonel's express orders, King Calakmul was returned in chains to Veracruz, and then unceremoniously thrown into the deepest dungeon below the Governor's palace. However, the matter did not rest with the Mayan leader's brutal incarceration. Capitalizing on having gained such a valuable hostage, and sensing an opportunity to increase his own personal wealth, the Spanish Governor had decreed that only on payment of a fabulous ransom in gold, would the Mayan leader be released unharmed.

Calakmul's tribal chiefs were amazed when they received the ransom demand. The Mayan people put no value on the abundant yellow metal, which they mined and smelted simply to make body ornaments and statues of their own bloodthirsty deities. If the cruel invaders were content with soft and worthless gold, the Mayan chieftains were only too happy to increase their mining, if it would return their God-like leader safely to them.

Don Rodrigo's cold eyes regarded the grey-haired nobleman that stood before him. Slowly, his thin face smiled.

'That is exactly what I wanted them to believe, Alveraz. You must understand that my rule here must be unequivocal and absolute.' He shook his head. 'I oversaw an execution the other morning. You know, before they died, the prisoner's attitude demonstrated to me that there is still a strong undercurrent of resistance to Spanish rule, and more particularly, to my own governorship within the region.' Don Rodrigo stood up and walked through the opened doors into the dazzling sunlight which bathed the wide veranda outside his office. He gazed across the thatched roofs and church spires of Veracruz, which shimmered and danced in the mid-day heat, then turned sharply back to his Adjutant. His face was sly.

'I will not permit these savages to reclaim their leader under any circumstances, Colonel.' As the Governor walked back into the cool shade of his office, he shook his head slowly. 'He would return to his people, lick his wounded pride and then raise a new army against us.' With narrowed eyes he continued, 'How long do you think before we would have a full-scale rebellion on our hands, eh?'

The veteran Colonel nodded grimly, 'Yes Excellency, I see your point.'

Don Rodrigo smiled again, this time with genuine pleasure. 'To kill the serpent of rebellion, first you must cut off its head. I plan to execute the Mayan King, destroy each of the rebellious tribal chiefs...and make a considerable profit from the whole enterprise.' He walked over to a small table on the other side of his palatial office. Pouring two glasses of ruby Madeira wine, he replaced the stopper in the crystal decanter, returned to the map table and said, 'Listen very carefully Alveraz.... This is what I want you to do...'

Chapter Six

The Master of the Sea Hawk stood hunched over the small table Quinn had swung down from the cabin wall. Spread before him was Humble Godshaw's latest additions to the library of coastal maps he had been drawing ever since their first landfall. Between violent bouts of seasickness, Master Godshaw produced highly detailed naval charts of more than two hundred miles of the Yucatan Peninsula's sinuous coastline. When the Sea Hawk returned to England, copies of the charts would be invaluable to other privateer captains, ordered to fresh adventure in the New World by their noble Queen.

Richard slowly traced the ink line of the coast with his finger. Engrossed, he stared intently at Godshaw's map, searching for anywhere suitable to hide both ships from patrolling Spanish ships, which by now, must be hunting for the missing Juliana. When his first officer gleefully reported a fortune in silver, loaded and securely locked in the Juliana's cavernous strong room, Richard doubted the Spaniards would write off such a valuable cargo, without first making a thorough search.

Anxiously peering over his shoulder, the map maker enquired. 'Err...Perhaps I can help? What exactly are you looking for, Captain?'

Richard turned from his studies for a moment. With his obvious eye for detail, perhaps the seasick mapmaker could be of use. He said,

'I need to find two things, Master Godshaw. When the rest of the water has been emptied from the forward cable tier, and we have full headway again, I need a suitable cove, somewhere nearby to put the Spaniards ashore. We don't have the manpower to guard more than seventy men who could attempt escape at any time, and also sail two damaged ships to a place of safety. Despite the Captain's promise, you can be sure that our prisoners would turn on us in an instant, if we dropped our guard.'

Humble Godshaw nodded. 'Yes of course, Sir Richard, I see...Err...You said you sought two things?'

Turning his attention back to Godshaw's charts, Richard nodded.

'Yes, indeed I did. The second consideration is rather more complicated. When we are no longer troubled by the Spaniards, we must find somewhere further along the coast to hide.' Richard leafed through the charts on the table, 'It will take at least a week for our carpenters and sail makers to effect sufficient repair to the Hawk and Juliana. If we are to elude the search parties which will surely come, we need somewhere both hidden and tidal to safely beach both vessels, so that not only can we make repairs with our feet dry between tides, but then we can easily re-float both ships when they are seaworthy again.'

The two men were interrupted by a sudden and powerful knock from the other side of the cabin door. It swung open as Quinn's bulk filled the narrow doorway.

'Beggin pardon, Sir Richard, Mister Howard reports that the cable tier is almost dry.'

'That's excellent news, Quinn.' With a triumphant grin, Richard slammed his fist onto the pile of parchments on the table in front of him. 'Give my compliments to Mister Howard, and tell him to get a tow rope on the Juliana... I'll be on deck shortly.' As Quinn withdrew and the cabin door closed Richard turned back to Humble Godshaw. 'You know what I require, Master Mapmaker.' His eyes narrowed. Urgently, the Hawk's Captain stabbed at the pile of finely drawn charts with his index finger. Another hour and the storm would be upon them. 'Find me what I need...and by the name of Christ man...do it quickly!'

* * *

56

'Get that damned beast back on its feet!'

Deep in the steaming Peruvian jungle, the long line of pack mules stalled yet again. In the damp oppressive heat, to the cacophony of animal and bird cries emanating from the impenetrable maze of lush green undergrowth surrounding them, a small group of sweating muleteers squelched through the bubbling waters of the latest stream, towards the stubborn animal which had abruptly halted the column. Angrily, they cursed and lashed at their charge, which had taken it into its stupid head to suddenly sit down on its hind legs in the cool of the thick mud beside the flowing water. Braying loudly, the mule obstinately refused to move another step, rebelling under the enormous weight of the bars of pure gold it carried.

With more than one hundred miles of tortuous winding trails still stretching ahead of them before arrival at the city of Veracruz, the mule-train's commander also cursed. It had taken almost two months to get this far from the distant Peruvian mines, and as always, he had been plagued with problems since beginning the long journey. The climate and terrain he reflected angrily to himself, were against them at every step. They began with more than a hundred beasts walking in single file, their bridles pulled by slaves and his tired muleteers and soldiers. During the journey, several beasts had slipped and fallen, crashing hundreds of feet to the rocks below, as the dangerous trail had led them through the high spine of mountains which separated Peru and Mexico. Each time a beast was lost, it had taken many hours to recover the precious load from each of the fallen animals, and as a result, and to the commanders growing consternation, the mule-train was now almost a week behind schedule.

His convoy of pack mules had been plagued with hit-and-run attacks from groups of unseen natives. The savages who lived in the jungle resented the white men's intrusion, and used their silent blow-pipes without warning, with deadly effect. They had brought down half a dozen mules during the journey, and to make matters worse, as many again of his men had also been killed by their poisoned darts. Panicked by each of these random attacks, his guards had discharged their muskets haphazardly into the jungle, but it would be a miracle if they had actually hit any of their unseen attackers. It seemed to him that there were more chances that the deafening noise of the muskets would startle and drive off the invisible attackers.

Dark clouds gathered quickly above the column, as the muleteers finally dragged the defiant mule to its feet. It began to rain again. Within moments of the first droplets announcing the rainstorm's arrival, the jungle canopy was pounded mercilessly by incessant driving rain. It cascaded and splashed down into the tangle of undergrowth below the lush canopy, and ran in rivulets along the tropical rainforest's floor. Most of his men had never experienced such torrential rain before entering the New World's interior for the first time, but all were once again drenched by the latest deluge. Within moments, visibility clamped down to just a few yards, and the track they traversed quickly disintegrated into a morass of glutinous mud, which gripped both hoof and boot alike, as the warm rain hammered down on them, falling unabated from the grey cloud-filled skies above. The soaking crew of the mule-train cursed the New World and its festering jungle as they slipped and blundered through the thick stinking mud.

The men had good reason to loath their surroundings. By day and night, the jungle was alive with a myriad of biting mosquitoes and formidable crawling insects, which constantly scuttled unseen in the leaf litter beneath their feet. Huge bird eating spiders bigger than a man's spread fingers lurked everywhere, deadly scorpions armed with needle-tipped stings and large poisonous vipers abounded under every twisted lattice of tree roots or decaying logs. Silently, they lay in wait for any creature, which failed to see them and blundered within striking

58

range. Buried in the leaf litter, silent and hungry, the venomous hunters waited; their skins painted with intricate camouflage patterns, which rendered them invisible to their unsuspecting prey.

One huge primordial horror lurked patient and invisible. The gigantic creature waited in ambush, concealed beneath the cool waters of the jungle's countless waterways; a nightmare beast who slithered silently into the waking dreams of both illiterate soldier and cultured nobleman alike. It was a terrifying constricting snake that wrapped its muscular coils, thicker than a man's torso, around any prey that its gaping mouth and needle-sharp teeth could seize. After a lightning strike, the deadly embrace of the powerful serpent monster squeezed the living breath from its dying victim, before swallowing its crushed prey whole.

Only after the protection afforded by the sign of the Cross, with mortal dread was its name even whispered by the superstitious soldiers of the mule-train. Heaven help the man who strayed within its extended striking range, they muttered. The name the men feared and murmured softly between them was *El Matatoro* - the Bull Killer...the giant 30-foot anaconda, which few men had seen and lived to tell the tale.

* * *

'By the mark...*Ten!*

The seaman perched on the bow of the Sea Hawk quickly hauled in the dripping lead weight attached to a length of wet knotted string. Without orders from his officers, the seaman swung the weight in an arc and released it again. It flew ahead of the privateer's bow wave and splashed into the wide rivers swirling depths.

'By the mark...*Ten!*

59

As the seaman continued to sound the depth below the Hawk's keel, her first officer turned anxiously and spoke to the ship's Master.

'Ten fathoms Captain. Still plenty of water below the Hawk.' The first officer glanced back towards the river delta, 'and we must but nearly a mile from the sea by now.'

Richard nodded. His plan to hide both ships by sailing up the wide river which Master Godshore's map had shown him was working. The river was wide and its current remained sluggish as the water drifted slowly towards the ocean. The storm's wind was with them, the Hawks sails filled with its angry breath. The rope between the two ships remained taut, as the Hawk towed the crippled Juliana behind it.

'By the mark...*Nine!*'

Honking their arrival, a flock of long necked water fowl suddenly swooped down from the heavens and landed with a watery hiss on the glassy surface of the river, close to the jungle covered bank beside the two silent ships. Abruptly, something howled high in the treetops as the bird settled noisily on the water. It was an unearthly booming howl which echoed across the wide river. The noise dramatically increased in volume as more of the creatures, concealed somewhere in the towering canopy, took up the cry.

Startled by the eerie chorus, several of Richard's seamen glanced towards their Captain as they nervously crossed themselves. One called out, with real fear in his voice.

'By the Holy Mother master, them's Devils out there!'

Richard smiled to reassure the frightened sailor. He shook his head,

'No, that's not the sound of Beelzebub's devils. It's just the call of strange animals that live in the jungle.' Richard's gaze swept towards the centre of the cacophony, emanating from somewhere deep in the treetops.

60

Busy tying off a rope, Quinn looked up. Hearing the exchange but not fully convinced, he muttered to himself. 'Aye, strange animals all right, in a damned strange land.'

Chapter Seven

'Only six fathoms now Sir Richard, the river is getting shallower by the minute.' William Howard glanced down at the muddy water as if to divine its hidden depth by sight alone.

It was an hour since the seaman had reported a steady call of ten fathoms. The current was still weak, but the storm had passed them by; the wind was noticeably beginning to slacken.

Richard nodded. Hampered with the added weight towing the Juliana, the Sea Hawk was now struggling to make headway, as the wind fell away against the slow but powerful flow of the muddy river, which drifted silently towards the delta and emptied into the ocean. With just 36 feet of water beneath the Hawks hull, there was now a serious danger of running aground in these uncharted waters, if they were unlucky enough to drift into a tangle of sunken logs or a hidden sand bar. With the Juliana in tow and drawing a deeper draught than the Hawk, Richard shielded his eyes from the sun's glare and searched either bank. The two ships had now sailed a little over two miles up the winding course of the broad un-named river. The temporary repair made hastily out to sea to the Hawk's bow was holding, but reports had reached Richard that more and more water had begun to seep back into the cable tier.

Having successfully put ashore the captured Spanish crew almost twenty miles back along the coast, now was certainly not the time to sink or become stuck fast on the river's muddy bottom, Richard mused. To make matters worse, the incoming tidal flow was beginning to slacken. To push further upstream was a tempting prospect, but without the wind, if either ship became stranded, they would be caught fast, out in the open and at the mercy of any searching Spanish ship, which might still discover them.

'*There!*' Richard suddenly shouted, pointing to a narrow tributary which dissected the wide river's bank ahead. Due to the lush overhang of the jungle, and sweeping curve of the riverbank, the smaller tributary had only just became visible. Triumphantly, Richard called over his shoulder. 'Three points to starboard, helmsman.'

'Aye-aye captain.'

The helmsman spun the wheel but without the wind behind them, as Richard had feared, the Hawk moved sluggishly. Beneath slack sails, lacking forward momentum, she was in danger of taking the Juliana with her as she drifted slowly back towards the ocean. Sir Richard cursed to himself and sighed deeply. He was running out of options. There was only one answer.

'Launch every boat we have from both ships, Will. I want every able-bodied man who can hold an oar in them. We'll pull the ships into cover.'

'But Captain, the current is beginning to ebb...its impossible!'

Richard snapped. 'Damn it man! We have no choice. If we don't find shelter soon we will be discovered...Would you rather the Spaniards take us as pirates and then face their torture and the fires of the Inquisition?'

The first officer's face paled momentarily then nodded without speaking. Silently, he cursed himself for his outburst. As he turned to begin issuing orders to the crew, Richard spoke again.

'And put a good man in the Juliana's crows-nest. Its mainmast is taller than the Hawk. Tell him to keep a sharp eye out, back towards the coastline.'

Men scattered to their posts to launch the Hawks two small boats. Snatching up a bullhorn, the first officer repeated the same order to unship their small boats, to the skeleton crew aboard the Juliana.

63

Alerted by the sudden commotion, Quinn's bulk lumbered onto the quarterdeck.

'Quinn, take the lead boat. We must pull our ships into stout cover.' Richard pointed towards the dark confines of the narrow tributary, 'I want both ships out of sight and hidden in there within the hour.'

Quinn raised an eyebrow and nodded. 'Aye master,' he spat into his hands and rubbed them together. 'With your permission, I'll go and join the others.'

A total of five small boats from the Hawk and Juliana, each crewed with the privateer's sailors, took up the slack of the long hemp ropes which connected each of them to the Hawks jutting bow. On a signal from Quinn, the crewmen readied themselves for the gruelling effort each of them knew was to come. They grumbled quietly to themselves and the others surrounding them, but each knew Sir Richard's order was their only chance. Some of the more experienced hands had seen this before. When their ship had become becalmed and trapped on a still windless ocean, their captains had ordered the crew into the boats, to tow the ship until their efforts found a wind. It could take days of agonising, back-breaking work before the wind suddenly stirred in the sails, and they could make good their escape.

'Put your backs into it lads. We hide the ships, or the Spaniards will find us...' Quinn roared. Bracing themselves, the scarred and tattooed sailors tightened their grip against the wooden oars. Each boat carried a coxswain, who would call the stroke to ensure the blades of each oar pulled together.

Seeing that all was ready, standing in the prow of the lead boat with his powerful arm raised, Quinn grinned wolfishly. 'It's time to earn your pay, lads.' Sweeping his arm forward he roared. 'Come on men, together now... *Heave!*'

Through gritted teeth, the sailors strained against the massive weight of the ships behind them. Heaving and cursing in equal measure, the men pulled with all their strength. The cool waters splashed by, as their wooden blades dug into the river's shimmering surface. Heave, recover, pause and pull. Heave, recover... The rhythm of the oars biting into the water beat its own tattoo. Within moments, each crewman was soaked with sweat in the hot humid atmosphere.

Slowly, the men's efforts and the loud encouragement of the boats coxswains began to work. Inexorably at first, the bow of the Hawk began slowly to move forward against the sluggish current of the wide river.

'That's it, come on lads, nearly there. Put your scurvy backs into it. Together now...*Heave!*'

'Steady now, let the wind take her.' Richard stood on the quarterdeck of the Hawk as he watched his men's efforts in the boats strung out before him. He turned to his first officer. 'Time is against us, Will. We'll see how far we can get up this branch, but I doubt we'll get too far.' His eyes swept the curtain of dense foliage, which lined both banks. Startled, a white bird suddenly launched itself into the air as the ships disturbed its roost. The cries of animals, concealed in the dense forest grew louder as the sweating crewmen made tortuous headway and slowly pulled the two wooden ships into deeper cover.

The impenetrable green walls of vegetation on either bank could hide an army of hostile natives, Richard mused, as he watched the jungle slowly close in around his ships. The flag displaying the Cross of St. George, which hung limply from the Hawk's stern, would mean nothing to those who called the jungle home. He was concerned that they might mistake him and his crew for Spaniards.

'It will be dark in an hour, and I want to anchor in midstream by nightfall. I'll not risk trying to tow at night on a narrow river like this,' he looked back towards the hidden ocean. 'We should be safely out of sight shortly. We'll watch the rise and fall of the tide before beaching as soon as we can after first light tomorrow.' Richard shook his head. 'I don't want to blunder about and find ourselves still stuck fast when repairs are complete, and it's time to re-float.' He pursed his lips and shrugged. 'I doubt we will have much room to play with, so best to take care. When we drop anchor, the men are to be rested and fed. An hour after dark, I want a small boat manned and launched. You will remain in command here, William. I'm going to make depth soundings around the Hawk and the Juliana, on either side of the river, right up to both shorelines...It should be safe to use torches to light our way. We're out of immediate danger of discovery here, and I doubt the Spaniards will risk searching for us at night, but we'll post sentries anyway.'

Richard walked towards the bow and watched the grunting efforts of Quinn and the small boats containing his labouring crews. Despite their hard work, progress was extremely slow, but yard by yard, the ships were inexorably moving further up the tributary. The river twisted and turned and was beginning to narrow, now with less than two hundred feet from the two ships to either shore.

The First Officer nodded. 'Yes Captain, that's all perfectly clear Sir, but how much further upstream do you intend to reconnoitre?'

Richard thought for a moment. 'Certainly no more than half a mile at most I think. That's if I can get the boat up that far. With the river narrowing, it will help increase the tidal flow, so ideally I'll be looking for a shallow sandbar at low tide if I can find one. I'll probably stop anyway when the mark goes down under four fathoms in the centre of the channel. I'll get Master Godshaw to come, and I'll take Quinn and a full rowing crew. With enough torchlight, Godshaw can draw a sketch map of the river's route as we progress, and I'll make sure he marks the depths accurately on the map as we sound the bottom with the weight.'

Richard's First Officer nodded. As he was about to leave and search out the mapmaker, Richard held up his hand and stopped him. His face was grim as Richard added.

'Tell Quinn to organise a rowing crew when you recall the boats and drop anchor in midstream tonight. I want an armed picket posted on both ships before it's fully dark.' Richard looked towards the edge of the river as it lapped gently against the shoreline. He stared intently at the solid green wall of jungle beyond. He saw nothing, but suddenly something shrieked an unearthly cry deep within the canopy. Ignoring it, Richard said. 'We don't know who or what's out there, and I don't want to be surprised...Tell the sentries to stay alert. You understand?'

The First Officer's anxious gaze also swept the tangled shoreline. He nodded gravely. 'Yes Sir Richard...trust me, I understand completely.'

Serenaded by a loud and incessant chorus of croaking frogs, hidden deep in the thick clumps of bulrushes which grew along both sides of the riverbank, the two torches mounted in the bow of the small boat flickered and danced as Richard ordered the next depth sounding. The torch's warm light spread a shimmering glow on the black waters as the crew pulled together against their oars. Here and there, twin dots of light on the surface mysteriously reflected pinpricks of light back towards the small boat as it sculled slowly forward into the night.

Quinn lay back and relaxed in the boat's stern. He kept a broad forearm resting on the long bar attached to the boat's rudder. Absently, he waved his other hand into the darkness in a vain attempt to drive off the ever-present mosquitoes which constantly buzzed around him and the other men in the boat. In front of him, seemingly oblivious to the flying insects sat Sir Richard and Humble Godshaw. Both men were crouched over the parchment spread before them which the mapmaker, by the flickering light of the torches, was busy adding more and more detail. The six crewmen were rowing steadily to Richard's order. Every twenty strokes they eased their oars momentarily as a new sounding was taken by Richard, and then carefully recorded on the map. The tributary had twisted and turned as the boat explored the narrowing river and so far, only one likely spot had been found to make the repairs. Richard was determined to seek out any more suitable places to beach the two ships. Having come this far, he and his small crew had long since lost sight of the Hawk and Juliana, which remained firmly anchored, further downstream.

In the bow, one of the crewmen angrily slapped at his cheek. From the corner of his mouth, Irish Jack whispered to the seaman sitting next to him.

'How much longer are we going to stay out here? I've had enough of this Malaki; I'm getting eaten alive.'

Malaki nodded. He whispered 'Yeah; you're right. Sooner we're back on the Hawk the bett....'

Suddenly, with a muffled thud the boat's bow lifted slightly as it came to an abrupt and jarring stop. The heavy impact sent a shockwave through the boat, throwing its occupants sprawling.

'*Bugger!* We've hit something, master.' Growled Quinn as he rubbed his back where he'd slid violently backwards and banged against the boats upright rudder bar. Angrily, he shouted. 'Irish Jack, get forward and see what we've hit.'

Cursing loudly as he disentangled himself from the man behind him, the scarred crewman obeyed. Irish Jack lifted his hand to the side of his head and felt a warm trickle of blood drip down from where he had cracked it on the bench behind him. Cursing his luck and staying low to retain his balance, Irish Jack edged forward in an awkward crouch to see what had caused the impact. The light of the torches flared across the rippling water, scarcely illuminating a broad lattice of jumbled logs, which lay ahead of the boat, tightly twisted and entwined together just inches below the obsidian surface of the river. In the poor light which had barely illuminated their progress, the boat's bow had rammed itself several feet over the nearest unseen trunks, which floated silently inches below the surface of the dark water.

'It's sunken logs!.... We're stuck on logs, Captain.'

'Well push us off then, damn you!' growled Quinn. He had not forgotten the sailor's earlier insolence. It seemed appropriate to give Irish Jack the task.

Muttering to himself, Irish Jack reached back and picked up a discarded oar. Swinging it over the bow, he tried to lever the boat free but to no avail, the boat was heavy and had ridden too far up onto the floating raft. Drops of blood dripped from his face into the water with muffled plops as he lent forward and heaved with all his strength. Hidden in the shadows, with the back of his calloused hand, Irish Jack wiped both blood and sweat from his brow as he twisted his head back towards the boat's stern. From the corner of his mouth, he hissed,

'This ain't a job for one man; I can't do it alone. Give us a hand will you, Malaki?'

With a reluctant snort, the nearest crewman joined him in the narrow bow and together, using their oars and grunting with effort, they tried in vain to push the boat free. It proved to be another useless struggle; the boat was stuck fast and stubbornly refused to budge.

Ignoring Quinn, Irish Jack wiped the blood clear of his eye and called back. 'It's no good Captain; we're still stuck fast!'

Richard exhaled deeply with frustration. His irritation was clear as he said, 'Quinn, get those two lazy devils out of the boat and onto the logs. We need to make the bow lighter anyway. They can push us clear; then jump back aboard.'

In the flickering torchlight, Quinn grinned as he nodded, 'Aye master...' He turned to the men waiting in the front of the boat. His Cornish accent growled at them, 'you heard the Captain; over the bow with you both and push us off.'

There were muffled sniggers among the remaining oarsmen.

'Quiet you dogs!' snapped Quinn angrily, 'or you'll all lend a hand. Don't make me come up there...get on with it, you two'.

Both Irish Jack and Malaki looked nervously at the dark waters surrounding them, and the tangle of barely floating logs. Reluctantly, knowing he had no choice but to obey his Captain's order, Malaki climbed carefully over the bow with a deep sigh and gently rested his foot on the closest log. Satisfied that it sank only a few inches and would bear his weight, he slowly twisted around and lowered himself onto the nearest part of the bobbing raft. To his relief, the lattice of logs held and the cool water barely lapped over his naked feet.

'Come on Jack, I can't do this on my own,' he hissed urgently.

Irish Jack blanched. There was a loud splash on the surface of the river, just beyond the spill of the torch light. Nervously, he whispered.

'I'm telling you Malaki.... there's... there's something out there.'

Ignoring his concerns, Maliki snapped back. 'Come on Jack, we haven't got all night.'

Tearing his eyes from the dark rippling water, Irish Jack snarled. 'All right damn you...I'm coming.'

His knuckles white, he reluctantly followed Malaki over the prow and onto the logs.

'Afraid of having a quick dip in the water then are we?' Malaki grinned to himself as he crouched down and braced his shoulder against the rough curve of the boat's bow.

As he got into position, Irish Jack comforted himself with the thought that he'd make Quinn pay dearly for this when they got back to the safety of the Hawk. There were plenty of dark corners below decks, where a man could wait with his knife held ready. He'd killed men before on other ships when they made the mistake of crossing him. One thing was for sure, Irish Jack thought; Quinn would not see dawn's light. He'd see to that. None of the crew still aboard the boat saw the feral grin on his face as he pressed down hard on the log below his foot. Putting his shoulder to the other side of the prow and grasping the top of the wooden hull, through gritted teeth Irish Jack hissed.

'Shut yer mouth and push, you lazy English bastard.'

At the two seamen strained against the hull, the logs on which they balanced slid backwards a few inches, before the tree trunks rammed into the others jammed behind them. With a slight jerk, the boat began to slide backwards. Sweat mixed with blood flowed freely from Irish Jack's deep cut as both men pushed with all their strength. The seaman's blood dripped into the water beneath him. Suddenly, there was a flash of silver in the water below. Irish Jack noticed the movement from the corner of his eye.

He grunted urgently. 'I told you, there is something in the water. I just...'

'Shut up and keep pushing, damn you! It's nearly free.'

Malaki was right. The boat was sliding faster now. With a grinding rumble and a sudden splash, the prow dropped off the logs and began to bob freely on the surface once again, to the muffled cheers of the relieved oarsmen who had remained on board the boat.

With a mighty effort, Irish Jack leapt forward and managed to grab onto the boat's prow. His face contorted with effort, he heaved himself up and slithered into a heap on the wooden planks which formed the floor of the boat.

Malaki was not so lucky. As the boat came free, his foot slipped on the wet log. He overbalanced, falling headlong into the water with a mighty splash. Instantly, he disappeared under the dark surface. As the laughing crewmen helped Irish Jack to his feet, Malaki surfaced several yards from the boat, loudly coughing up at least some of the scummy water he had swallowed.

Water dripped from his hair, 'Stop laughing you bastards, and help me back aboard,' he snarled angrily.

No-one noticed a lightning flash of silver in the water beside him, or the unexpected blur of many other quicksilver streaks. As Malaki began to swim back towards the boat, the peaceful night was rent when he suddenly grimaced and let out a piercing scream of pain and terror. Malaki thrashed frantically at something unseen, as the water began to boil and froth around him. The men aboard the boat sat frozen for a moment, their minds trying to process the horror which had suddenly exploded in the water before them. A heartbeat later, there was terrified panic aboard the boat as the crewmen cried out. Richard was first to shake himself free. Frantically, he grabbed an oar and thrust it out towards the seaman known simply as Maliki.

'Here! Grab onto it man,' he thundered, but Malaki was out of reach, and it was too late.

Dark blood pooled around the thrashing seaman; the water surrounding him foamed pink in the flickering torchlight. The helpless sailor continued to shriek with agony as the piranha pressed home their frenzied attack. As Malaki splashed and rolled in the water, some of the red-bellied fish were heaved from the water. As big as house bricks, they gnashed their razor-sharp teeth and thrashed powerful tails in a tumult of spray and blood, before disappearing back into the blood-stained depths.

Richard thrust the useless oar aside and rose up. Quinn saw his master rise and leapt forward. Grabbing Richard's arm in a vice-like grip, Quinn frantically shouted. 'No master, don't go into the water...' Keeping his eyes fixed on his anguished Captain, Quinn's voice softened to a low growl as he shook his shaggy head, 'it's too late, you cannot save him, master.'

72

His face blazing, Richard whirled on Quinn, but in that moment, he knew his servant was right. With a final piercing shriek, Malaki slipped below the surface and vanished. His frantic screaming and splashing were suddenly replaced with just a swirling eddy in the dark waters, and eerie, empty silence. The water rippled where the tattooed seaman had disappeared. A piece of ragged, blood-stained shirt floated to the surface, but that was all which remained. The men aboard the boat stared silent and frozen in the moments after their crew mate had disappeared. Each of them was held in the grip of pure horror as they stared at the forlorn scrap of material and the stain of spreading ripples on the still water. No-one spoke or moved until Richard cleared his dry throat and quietly said.

'Malaki has gone, men. The devil fish have taken him, and we can't help him....' Nodding towards his ashen faced mapmaker, he sadly added. 'We are done here lads. It's time to pack up and get back to the living, aboard the Hawk.'

Chapter Eight

The men's mood was sombre as the sun began to rise next morning. Word had spread like wildfire among the crew of Malaki's horrific demise. The superstitious sailors crossed themselves and grumbled to each other, beneath the flickering light of tallow candles on the mess deck, as they hammered their hardtack biscuits on the small tables before them, to remove the weevils.

In the shadows of the cramped mess deck, Irish Jack had decided to wait, before settling his score with Quinn. A blade in the back would bring an enquiry, and his Captain, Jack thought, was too clever by half. The mutual dislike which simmered between Irish Jack and the master gunner was widely known aboard ship; Fingers would point, and other scores would be settled under the harshness of naval law. He had no intention of being found guilty and hanged, strung high up in the yards for murder. Jack's mind was made up. He'd bide his time. There would be an opportunity; they'd be alone, sooner or later. He wanted his story believed, and no witnesses to see him finish it between them.

Having recovered from the terror which had coursed through his veins the night before, Irish Jack returned to his usual insolent bluster. His upper lip curling with disgust, he looked down at the crawling weevils, which he had just dislodged from the rock-hard ship's biscuit. The revulsion remained on his scarred face, as the tiny maggoty creatures tried to crawl away and hide under the small portion of salted fish on his platter. Even that had gone bad. It was tinged with green, pungent with the reek of decay.

'Even the stinking food is rotten in this filthy place,' he snarled, and dropped the rocklike biscuit onto his stained pewter plate with a clatter. Scratching a fleabite on his shoulder, he

74

looked up at his mess-mates, 'Malaki has gone, so who is going to be next, that's what I want to know?'

Miserably, his crew mates nodded and mumbled their agreement. Their ship was cursed; one muttered. A white-haired old sailor named Silus suggested a Jonah aboard, who would bring them nothing but bad luck. Younger sailors deferred to old Silus' wisdom, after his lifetime at sea. Whispered complaints were common, even aboard the happiest of ships, but there was almost an underlying hint of mutiny in the collection of their grumbling words.

Crammed under the low beamed wooden ceiling, Quinn's bulk sat hunched in a corner of the mess deck. He was deeply troubled by Silus' prediction, and the men's low morale. So far from home, if spirits continued to plummet, things might turn ugly for the officers and the ship's Master. With loudmouths like Irish Jack stirring up the crew, there could be serious trouble aboard if these dark mutterings continued unabated below decks. Thoughtfully, he bit down into his own breakfast of hardtack. Quinn shifted uncomfortably and listened as the seamen continued to grumble, but said nothing. Then, a half-smile crept across the shadows of his face, as an idea occurred to him. From his darkened corner, he growled,

'Our watch is due; we're on deck in five minutes, lads. I'll speak to the Captain before we start work. Tell you what; let me see if I can make things right…'

'Beggin pardon, Sir Richard. Can I have a word, Sir?'

Standing on the quarterdeck, bathed in the welcome light of the early morning, Quinn touched his forelock and waited patiently for his master to turn and speak to him.

Richard had been lost in thought, staring gloomily across the mist shrouded river.

In these quiet lonely moments, he brooded with deep melancholy, as thoughts flowed back to his days on Malta, and his beloved Miriam. In his sorrow, his mind constantly relived that one awful moment, during the last great battle against the Turks. Surrounded by the clash of steel and roar of cannon, the woman he loved so much had been cruelly torn from him by a sniper's bullet. As Miriam fell, he had seen it as no more than a cruel twist in the raging battle, but shortly afterwards, things had changed forever. His mind became dark and murderous, as he pictured the leering face of Don Rodrigo Salvador Torrez. The Spanish nobleman had a wounded Richard at his mercy just after the battle. He openly gloated as he boasted that it was he who had fired the fateful shot; his assassin's bullet was meant for Richard. Quinn had inadvertently saved Richard's life that day, but cruel fate and his uncle's intervention had removed any chance of Richard getting the revenge his soul craved. The bitter wound of Richard's broken heart remained raw and open. Vengeance would only be served with Don Rodrigo's skewered body on the end of Richard's sword. Then at last, Richard could begin to mourn, and find relief and gradual healing.

His heart heavy, Richard turned. With a sigh, he said sadly,
'Yes Quinn, what is it you want?'

Apart from the guards on the Juliana, the entire crew of the Sea Hawk were assembled on the gun deck, hushed and waiting expectantly for their Captain to speak. Standing above them on the quarterdeck, Richard cleared his throat and stared down into the fearful faces below. With a nod to his officers, he began,

'As you all know lads, we lost a member of the crew last night. It was a tragedy, but no-one's fault. Maliki died in this strange land, attacked by the savage fish which live in this river. It is a sorry lesson for us all. We're here and must affect repairs to our ships, but at the same time exercise extreme caution while we work. None of us have ever been on land in the New World before, and we must protect ourselves while our ships remain here under repair. I have ordered a permanent guard, armed with

76

muskets, to be posted to protect our work parties when we go into the jungle to cut timber. When they begin their repairs, our ship's carpenters will also be guarded while they work on the Juliana's rudder and the Hawk's bow.'

The crewmen muttered together, feeling a little reassured by the protection Richard was organising. Their Captain held up his hand to quell further muttering between the crew.

'We don't know who or what hides in this great forest, so at no time is any man permitted to enter the jungle alone, by day or night. Quinn will organise work details to gather timber shortly, and some of you will assist the carpenters making their repairs. With luck, if we work hard we should be clear and ready to sail in five or six days; a week at the most,' Richard paused for a moment, then continued as he rested his hand on the pommel of his sword, 'once we are seaworthy again men, we will have two fine ships to prick our enemies. After that, we can start looking for Spaniards once again, and of course...' he grinned, 'help ourselves to their gold.'

The Hawk's master was rewarded with a crowd of grinning faces, looking up from the gun deck. The lure of rich booty always helped raise the men's spirits and forget their troubles, but Richard did not finish with them quite yet. He had something else to say, which he knew would sit well with his crew. Smiling, he added,

'Ah yes, one more thing, men. Quinn suggested something to me this morning. When enough timber is collected, not all of you will be required to work on the repairs.' He cast a hand towards the jungle. 'These lands must abound with wild pig and deer. What say you to a hunting party, lads, and some fresh meat in your bellies?'

To a man, sick of the foul, tainted remains at the bottom of the ship's provision barrels, the crew cheered, roaring their approval at Quinn's idea. Grinning broadly, several of the old hands whooped and slapped his powerful shoulders, to register

77

their agreement and delight at armed parties hunting in the jungle.

Richard allowed his men a moment of celebration, and then fixed his gaze on his giant servant.

'Get the men to their labours, Quinn. There's work to be done, and plenty of hungry bellies to fill.'

Chapter Nine

Dotted by sweating sailors, the gloom and shadows of the jungle floor were filled with the sound of their efforts, as the grunting seamen swung felling axes, which thudded into the bases of great hardwood trees, sending fat white woodchips flying in all directions.

One tree already was felled, and surrounded by seamen working in pairs synchronised together, drawing great bow saws back and forth across its gnarled trunk. As a fresh section was released from the trunk, it was hastily rolled away towards the small tidal bay nearby, where the Hawk and Juliana were safely beached. The Hawk's carpenters were busy on the riverbank, splitting and shaving the newly arrived timber into the planks and spas they needed to make both ships seaworthy again.

Standing in the jungle gloom with hands on hips; the long handle of a heavy axe resting against his broad thigh, Quinn breathed deeply as he caught his breath. Wiping the sweat from his brow, his eyes wandered upwards, following the tall trunk before him, until it disappeared into the leafy tangle of the canopy, high above. To his simple, uncluttered mind, it seemed the green mantle reached out and touched the low clouds, and supported the very heavens beyond. Smiling to himself at the childish fancy, he remembered a story his mother had once told him, as they sat huddled together one cold, rainy night, in front of the blazing hearth within their tiny Cornish miner's cottage, so many long years ago. Idly, he hoped the sky would not fall on him when the tree finally succumbed to his axe. With a snort at his foolishness, Quinn dismissed childhood fairy-tale and returned his gaze to the livid wound he had so far hacked from the stout trunk. Satisfied with his progress over the past thirty minutes, Quinn spat into his palms, rubbed them vigorously together, and got back to work.

Having marked the trees he wanted, before he returned to the riverbank, Richard was busy walking the perimeter, checking that his sentries were alert.

'Seen anything?' he enquired to the last of his guards. The sailor sniffed, and hefted his musket across his shoulder. Tugging on his forelock, the sailor shook his head,

'Nothing Captain, save some monkeys chattering up in yonder trees.' With his free hand, the sentry slapped irritably at something buzzing behind his neck, 'but I've seen plenty of mosquitoes.'

Richard grinned at the man's discomfort, then suddenly slapped at his own cheek. Wiping the sticky mess on his breeches, he said, 'better mosquitoes than leaches though, eh?...Make sure you stay awake and keep a sharp lookout,' he nodded towards the musket over the man's shoulder, 'and don't be afraid to use that, if you have to.'

The sentry nodded nervously, his eyes flicking apprehensively towards the shaded gloom of the jungle, just feet beyond their reach.

'Aye Captain, don't worry, you'll soon know when there's trouble, all right; I'll blast the first head-hunting heathen face I see...' The sentry's eyes narrowed dangerously, 'by God, I will!'

Richard grinned; 'Let's hope then, for their sake, you don't see any.'

Nearby, in the little cove where the Hawk and Juliana lay moored close beside each other, sailors not ordered to tree cutting or sentry duty that morning, hammered or sawed around the damaged stern or bow of the two ships. Under the watchful eye of Richard's master carpenter, and his small team of carpenter's mates, construction of a long, straight makeshift jetty was progressing well. All the while, the seamen remained fearful of the dark water beneath them, where they were sure the unseen devil fish still lurked.

Their temporary repairs holding, both vessels rose and fell beside each other, as the tide ebbed and flowed. Wooden barrels, long since emptied of provisions, had been brought up from the holds and put over the side. Once securely fastened in place, they supported the almost finished floating dock, so that repairs to bow and stern could begin shortly, even at low tide, when the ships' keels settled on the bottom and became entombed in the thick riverbed mud.

One end of the jetty almost reached the riverbank. The Master carpenter's plan called for the last fifteen feet between jetty and bank to be left unfinished. During the days ahead, a long plank would link them, and, like a drawbridge, could be raised at night to avoid unwelcome visitors.

A bored sailor, armed with a long musket, stood guard at the end of the floating dock, as it bobbed gently on the falling tide. He snapped to attention when he saw his Captain appear from the jungle curtain. Richard strode towards the gangplank, as several crewmen close by were stacking long fat logs, before each was sorted by the carpenters, and the slow process of sawing and shaping them down into individual, tight-fitting planks began. Richard spied his master carpenter standing halfway down the jetty, taking preliminary measurements for the Juliana's replacement rudder. Engrossed in his work, he was using a knotted string, suspended from the Juliana's high stern deck, and held by one of his assistants. Beside him, Humble Godshaw, quill in hand, was studiously transferring the measurements onto a parchment sketch of the planned replacement. To Richard's surprise, the mapmaker looked well. His face was pink and glowing; lacking its usual green tinge. Richard smiled to himself. Perhaps they'd make a sailor of him yet. The smile faded quickly. There again, he thought, perhaps not.

'How goes it, Silus?'

81

The carpenter turned, when he heard his captain's question,

'It goes well, Sir Richard. I have the measurements I need for the Hawk's bow already, and we've nearly finished with the new rudder's design.'

Richard's face clouded suspiciously. Eager for good news, he enquired, 'How soon will both ships be seaworthy?'

Silus pondered the question for a moment, and then he said,

'We should have enough timber out of the forest by nightfall, Sir. We can begin properly shaping and steaming the planks for the Hawk's bow tomorrow morning. It will take at least another day to fit them all, and then we'll need to caulk the seams, of course, to make sure she's good and watertight.'

Richard nodded, 'what about the damaged spa in the cable tier?'

The old carpenter's brow furrowed, 'I'm hoping that I can repair the split section, rather than replace it. To be honest Captain, I won't know until we strips out the damage planks in the bow, and I can take a really good look at the extent of the spa's damage.

Richard sighed. He had hoped for better news, but nevertheless had expected the carpenter's caution,

'So at least another day, if the spa needs replacing?' he said expectantly.

The carpenter shook his head. His expression didn't offer a morsel of comfort,

'Hmm. More likely two but realistically three days to be safe, Captain.'

Richard scowled, 'what about the Juliana's rudder?'

Silus' face brightened a little, 'Why, that should take no more than two days' work to cut and build Sir, and another day to fit.'

'So we are beached for at least a week then?'

Silus smiled weakly. 'Barring anything going wrong, a week should be enough, Captain.'

Richard rubbed his hand across his mouth and cursed silently to himself. A week was a long time, and he had hoped for less, but before he had been put ashore, the Juliana's master let slip that the Spanish treasure convoy wasn't due to sail for two weeks.

'Very well, Master Carpenter. I'll see to it that you have all the men you need.' Richard's eyes darkened. One week then, and not a single minute more.'

As the sun cleared the eastern horizon next morning, Richard and a small hunting party assembled on the riverbank. A mist hung across the river; it had drifted unseen in the night into the cove, where the two ships remained at anchor. Translucent tendrils of white gossamer swirled about the men, and disappeared silently past them into the jungle. All around, hidden high in the canopy, shrill birdsong and the raucous howling of strange creatures bade welcome to the morning's sun. The clamour filled the hunter's ears; sharpening straining senses, and sending stout hearts racing.

To feed starving families, some of the assembled sailors had turned their hands to poaching in earlier years. Here and now, their past experiences brought little comfort. These weren't the lush oak and sweet chestnut glades of England, or the pastures of green and rolling downs of Devon and Sussex. The blaring chorus around them was a stark fanfare of the strange and alien world they were about to enter. Eyes wide with apprehension, Richard's men stared about them, searching for the merest glimpse, or slightest hint of movement in the solid wall of primeval jungle which awaited them. Several sailors nervously crossed themselves, as they waited impatiently for the captain's signal, to begin the hunt.

When Quinn had chosen six of the Hawk's best men to form the hunting party the previous evening, they had preened, bragged and strutted before their shipmates. Now, surrounded by dense jungle and sinister swirls of early morning mist, their previous bluster was gone; they stood together nervously muttering between themselves as they waited for the order to proceed. Somehow, the thought of spending the day beginning repairs on the two ships had become suddenly more appealing.

Each man wore a ship's cutlass jammed in his belt, and carried either a longbow or musket. The bowmen wore quivers filled with fletched; iron-tipped arrows secured at their hips; the musketeers wore broad belts diagonally across their chests. Small individual leather pouches filled with powder and shot hung from the cross belts, and could easily be accessed when reloading was necessary. The men fingered their weapons nervously at the reality of unseen danger, but were buoyed just a little by the thought of fresh meat in their growling bellies. No man wore steel plate or iron helmet. Richard judged it too hot and humid to carry the heavy burden of armour. This was, Richard reasoned, merely an expedition to find fresh meat. He wanted his men relaxed, as they spent the morning quietly sweeping the jungle; searching out animal trails, and the game Richard hoped would be using them.

When he had risen that morning, Richard had left William Howard in command. He was a capable and experienced officer, who would soon be elevated to the rank of captain of his own ship. His orders were simple. The repairs must begin at first light, and a careful watch must be kept for the unseen dangers which surrounded them. Now, before they set off, Richard turned and calmly said to Quinn and the others,

'We'll keep a sharp lookout all around as we enter the forest, men. We search for wild pig or deer, but we just don't know what else lurks in there. We must be patient and exercise caution. Once we find an animal trail, we'll follow it to water.

84

We should find plenty of game gathered around a waterhole, wherever we may find one.'

Each of the seamen nodded. Tongues flicked across their dry lips as Richard added, 'Remember men; there may well be savages in there who call this jungle home. We look for no fights, but be prepared to defend yourself, if I give the order.'

Satisfied they all understood the plan, and the dangers that might await them, Richard ordered his men to follow on in single file. Drawing his cutlass, the Hawk's master chose a direction, and ignoring the deafening, discordant cries around them in the forest, began slicing through the undergrowth; hacking a path through hanging lianas and dense undergrowth, which sprouted everywhere from the jungle floor.

The small group moved off behind Richard and were quickly swallowed up by the swirling mist, as they disappeared one by one into the shadows and gloom of the waiting jungle.

Chapter Ten

'Is everything prepared, exactly as I ordered?'

Colonel Alveraz nodded. 'Yes Excellency, the men are in position, and I have just received a report from the guard commander at the city's main gate that the native convoy of one hundred wagons containing King Calakmul's ransom are outside the walls, awaiting your permission to enter Veracruz.'

Don Rodrigo sighed to himself. How easy it was to fool these simple savages. In less than an hour, his devious plan would be completed. The price of freedom was truly a King's ransom; he thought with a sly smile. His largest treasury storeroom was to be completely filled to its high ceiling with gold. That was the payment he demanded, for the return of the Mayan King to his people.

Don Rodrigo had sent word that the ransom must be presented today, on the holy day of the festival of St. Teresa. He had invited all of Calakmul's surviving nobles to share the feast, as a sign of the Governor's forgiveness for their earlier insurrection. A promise had been made to the Mayan chieftains. It declared that provided they all attended; gifts from the Governor would be bestowed upon them, and peace would exist forever more between the Spanish Empire and the Mayan people. The pact would exist from the moment the ransom was paid in full, and the King was, as promised, given back to his people.

'Has Calakmul been removed from his dungeon?'

'Yes, Excellency. He remains shackled of course, and is currently under close guard, as you ordered.'

The smile returned to the Don's thin face. Dismissing Alveraz, he strode quickly from the audience chamber, into the bright sunshine which bathed the broad veranda outside. Don Rodrigo came to a stop, and rested his hands on the stone

86

balustrade. Breathing deeply in the warm scented air, he leaned forward and stared down into the cobbled courtyard below. A high wall of fat, iron hooped barrels lined one side. A dismounted officer stood beside them, waiting...

Formed up in a long column directly below him, the armoured troopers of the cavalry escort sat patiently on their horses, their lance pennants fluttering in the gentle breeze. The sun glinted on their polished helmets and burnished breastplates. They were waiting for the order to proceed to the main gate; and escort the Mayan nobles, and the King's ransom, back to the Governor's palace.

Satisfied that all was in order, and his preparations were ready, Don Rodrigo called down to the cavalry officer at the head of the escort,

'You may proceed, Captain.'

The echoing clatter of iron-shod hooves faded as the last troopers in the column rode away towards the city walls. High on the veranda, the Governor of Veracruz felt his pulse quicken with anticipation as he turned his attention back to the lone officer standing beside the barrels. Don Rodrigo lifted his arm above his head and dropped it suddenly. The watching officer spied the signal and returned it in acknowledgement. Grinning, the artillery captain turned, and disappeared behind the silent wall of wooden barrels...

* * *

Quinn was taking his turn at the head of the file. He swung his powerful arm, and slashed at the undergrowth for the hundredth time with his Arab scimitar. Richard was walking slowly behind him. He marvelled at his manservant's reserve of seemingly endless energy. The others had become exhausted after cutting for just ten minutes; Quinn had spent double that in the vanguard, blazing their trail, but exhibited no obvious sign of fatigue or strain.

After almost an hour of cutting a path through the virgin jungle, despite Quinn's energetic efforts, progress remained agonisingly slow. Many of the vines which draped haphazardly across their path were protected with vicious thorns and needle-sharp spines, which snagged and stabbed through the flesh of the unwatchful. To men used to salt air, and a rolling deck beneath their feet, the jungle floor seemed alive with huge horned beetles, scorpions and the biggest spiders any of the hunting party had ever seen. Thankfully, with the noise the men were making, poisonous snakes which lay in ambush were disturbed before they could strike; the reptiles hissed angrily and slithered away into deeper leaf litter as the hunting party approached.

To add to the misery of the jungle, the hot, humid air was filled with mosquitoes, flies and tiny bees, which buzzed in irritating clouds around the faces of the sweating men. Beneath a still raucous canopy, which allowed only narrow beams of sunlight to penetrate the shadows and half-light on the jungle floor, Richard could see his men's moral was slipping. They cussed and swore angrily at the jungle, and given the slightest provocation, each other. Richard offered up a silent prayer that they would soon enjoy some well needed luck.

Suddenly, Quinn held up his hand and stopped; his crashing progress coming to an abrupt halt. He turned back towards his master. Grinning broadly, Quinn pointed at the ground just ahead, and barked triumphantly.

'Ha! Sir Richard – *Look here!*'

Hoping his prayer was answered, Richard walked forward to see what had excited his giant servant. Sure enough, Quinn had found what they had been searching for. The massive Cornishman had stumbled across a well-worn animal trail, which cut diagonally across their line of march. Although just wide enough for a man to walk along, the track was well defined, and judging by the myriad of fresh cloven hoof prints pressed into the soft loam, the track was regularly used by the very animals the hunting party sought.

Richard slapped Quinn's muscular shoulder. 'Well done, you rascal; that's exactly what we seek.' Richard turned to the rest of his sullen men.

'Here lads; Quinn's found the track we seek.' To raise their spirits, and encourage them still further, Richard commanded, 'step forward now men; see for yourselves…'

* * *

A loud peal of trumpets announced the arrival of the Mayans, and the long convoy of rumbling carts which slowly followed them.

Dressed in their finest ceremonial attire and resplendent in gaudy feathered headdress, more than eighty Mayan nobles advanced, two by two, into the walled courtyard in front of the Governor's palace.

Venerated by their people for their sage wisdom, most were white-haired and very old. Oblivious to the barrier of great age, their proud, defiant bearing suggested their hearts retained their warrior status. Carrying gold trimmed jade axes, which symbolised both power and status in Mayan society, they were a colourful and magnificent sight. These nobles had walked freely into the viper's nest of the hated iron-shirts, as representatives of their people and indeed, their very civilisation. None showed fear at entering the enemy's city, however. Under Mayan law, their safety was assured. A sacred pact had been entered into to release their King, and they had come to Veracruz to honour it.

Don Rodrigo Salvador Torrez, King Phillip II's Provincial Governor of Veracruz, his most senior land and naval officers,

Bishop Acosta and priests of the Inquisition watched the procession of native nobles silently enter the courtyard below. This would be a defining moment of my governorship, mused the cruel Spanish Don, as he sipped chilled wine and chatted casually with the others while the distinguished gathering waited for the conclusion of the morning's entertainment.

As each richly dressed Mayan stopped and turned to face the high veranda, Don Rodrigo and the others could see both cold defiance and deepest loathing in the coal-black eyes staring back at them. Don Rodrigo fought to suppress a cruel smile, as the last nobles arrived and silently took up their positions. The carts containing the King's ransom did not enter the courtyard. Instead, under the cracking whips of their drovers, the teams of oxen the Governor had ordered into the jungle days earlier pulled their heavy burdens towards the great storeroom, deep inside the Governor's heavily guarded treasury building.

Seeing that all were finally assembled, and the last of the carts had rolled away, Don Rodrigo stared his entourage into silence, and then nodded towards one of his more junior officers, who seeing the Governor's signal, barked out an order,

'Bring out the prisoner!'

The young captain snapped his fingers. With hands securely bound behind him, a pitiful man dressed in rags was half-carried and half-dragged by two burly Spanish soldiers into the sunlight, from the gloom of the Governor's audience chamber. In stark contrast to the fine raiment's below, the prisoner was emaciated and filthy. The soldiers frogmarched the Mayan King to the stone balustrade, and held his rolling head firmly upright, for all below to see.

There were immediate mutterings of amazement and horror from the courtyard, as the nobles realised the man so cruelly treated above them was Calakmul. Someone among the crowd of nobles shouted angrily,

'They treat our King like a common criminal!'

Don Rodrigo's pinched face broke into a smug, satisfied grin, as one of his house-boys, standing behind his shoulder translated the furious cry to him.

The Governor strode to the balustrade, and held his arms aloft. He roared one word, which need no translation,

'SILENCE!'

The crowd of angry nobles hushed, as the echoes died away. Don Rodrigo beckoned his native houseboy to his side, and ordered him to translate the words he was about to speak.

'From your master, his most Catholic majesty, King Phillip of Spain, greetings…'

The boy translated, as Don Rodrigo turned, and rested his hand on Calakmul's shoulder.

'This man, like all of you, is guilty of gross and vile insurrection against your lawful King, who was anointed by almighty God to rule over you.' The boy translated, and the Governor continued, 'Under Spanish law, there is only one punishment for this most foul and heinous crime against his majesty.'

While the houseboy spoke Don Rodrigo's words in his native Mayan tongue to the assembled nobles, the Governor signalled a hooded man to step forward. When his official executioner stood firmly behind the manacled King, Don Rodrigo's cruel eyes narrowed as he hissed, 'Carry out Calakmul's lawful death warrant signed by my own hand…*Garrotte him!*

With a feral grin hidden beneath his cowl, the executioner quickly slipped the hemp noose he had held behind his back over the doomed King's head. Adding a wooden handle through the loop of rope, he began to twist it. The rope quickly tightened around Calakmul's neck, crushing his throat, and cutting off the flow of air to his windpipe. The King's eyes bulged as he fought to snatch a last breath, but it was too late. The dying King's

91

struggles became weaker, as the executioner added a last few twists to his garrotte's handle.

Don Rodrigo looked on with satisfaction, as his orders were carried out. His eyes flicked back towards his grace, the most reverend Bishop Acosta. The Bishop looked on with disdain, in silence. Agreement on both the expediency, and necessity, of the King's execution had been reached the previous night during a private supper between the two men, after a percentage of the ransom's worth had been agreed between them both, which would be quietly donated by the Governor, on behalf of his distant monarch, to Holy Mother Church, for what was agreed would be the furtherance of God's work among the heathens in the New World.

The executioner was shielded from the courtyard by the stone balustrade and Calakmul. With a last strangled gasp, the King's throttled body went limp in the hands of the guards, who still held him firmly upright.

Satisfied that all was proceeding to plan, led by the Governor, the observers withdrew from the balcony, and took cover inside the palace. A single peal of a Spanish trumpet rent the air, sending a signal to the soldiers who crouched behind the barrel wall.

As their King's lifeless body was hurled into the courtyard below, the barrel wall suddenly collapsed, exposing the gaping muzzles of six, eight-pounder cannon. Each was loaded with deadly grapeshot. Startled by the clatter of the falling barrels, the nearest Mayan nobles turned towards the commotion and instantly realised it was a trap. Before they could draw breath and shout a warning, the captain commanding the battery dropped his sword arm, sealing their fate forever with a single bellowed word.

Fuego!'

Chapter Eleven

The wild pig grunted contentedly, as its broad snout ploughed through the mud beside the silver pool. It snuffled happily as it searched out tasty bulbs and roots buried in the ooze, oblivious to the fact that it was being watched by men with hunger growling in their bellies.

Richard and his men had cautiously followed the animal trail downhill through the jungle for almost a mile, until they abruptly came across the wide clearing, and the waterhole in its centre. Richard had ordered his men to stay low in cover, while he and Quinn inched forward to get a better view.

Apart from the solitary boar, there were several small deer standing head down with legs splayed at the water's far edge, drinking contentedly from the sparkling pool. A carpet of dazzling butterflies fluttered and settled on the other bank of the pool, close to Richard and Quinn, feeding on the salts contained in the soft, mineral-rich mud. The scene was tranquil, until suddenly alert; the biggest of the deer lifted its head. It anxiously sniffed the air. Ears pricked and twitching; the little stag suddenly let out a coughing bark, and dashed back into the jungle, closely followed by several smaller does', and the squealing pig.

'They must have caught our scent, master,' growled Quinn.

Richard heard hunger and the twang of bitter disappointment in his servant's voice. Feeling confused by the animal's startled reaction, Richard said softly,

'No, Quinn; the air remains still around us. Our scent couldn't possibly have carried to the other side of the pool that quickly.' With furrowed brows, Richard continued to stare towards the deserted waterhole, until he shook his head and whispered, 'No, something else must have disturbed the animals, and put them to flight.'

93

Both men continued to spy on the pool. Moments later, movement on the upstream side of the stream which fed the watering hole caught their eyes. A line of dark-skinned men broke cover. All of them carried bows or spears. Tied to a pole, balanced between two of the men's shoulders, the limp body of a wild pig hung suspended from it. Unaware they were being watched; the small party followed their leader and picked their way carefully along the water's edge, before disappearing moments later back into the jungle.

Quinn watched in silence as the last man was enveloped by the undergrowth. Then he hissed, 'Must be the savages you warned us about. A native hunting party perhaps, master?'

Richard was not so sure. It was certainly a hunting party, but there were negroes among the group, and the leader, taller than the rest, looked heavily sun-burnt, and to Richard's surprise, his features at a distance anyway, looked distinctly European.

Intrigued by this strange turn of events, Richard waved Quinn back towards the others. When they re-joined the other crewmen, Richard spoke softly,

'There's something strange going on here, lads. We've just seen a small hunting party of some sort break cover over on the far side of the pool, but they were not local savages, and they certainly were not Spaniards.'

Confused like the others, one of the crewmen asked, 'Then who exactly were they, Captain, pirates?'

Richard shook his head, 'I've no idea, but I think we need to know.'

He considered for a moment, then; his mind made up, Richard said. 'Quinn and I will follow them, while you men stay here and hunt the game which favours this waterhole. Use your bows to make a kill, but for God's sake don't fire a musket, whatever you do. Those men might be camped close by, and will hear the shot. We don't know how many there are, if they are

94

friendly…or allies of the Spaniards.' Richard nodded towards his manservant, 'Come on Quinn,' he whispered, 'let's get after them, while we still have plenty of daylight.'

* * *

As the last of the riddled bodies was loaded onto carts by his soldiers down in the blood-soaked courtyard, Don Rodrigo was sitting at his desk, inside the cool shade of his ornate office. Initial reports from the treasury building suggested that the quota of gold demanded as ransom would more than fill the storeroom. Perhaps, at last, his plans were beginning to turn the tide of misfortune, which had threatened to drown the House of Torrez in a sea of debt.

Rubbing tired eyes, satisfied too that he had finally cut off the head, and crushed further Mayan rebellion forever, Don Rodrigo considered his next move carefully, in the drive to increase production in the mines throughout his vast jungle province.

He could, of course simply order his guards to be more liberal with the lash, and work the already emaciated army of slaves to death; but he rejected the idea as counterproductive. Don Rodrigo needed a workforce capable of digging out the ore; killing them with overwork might perhaps provide a short-term increase in tonnage of ore mined, but would mean, overall, a shortfall in production as his workforce expired. Increasing their meagre rations would cost too much.

Manpower was always both problem and key, but finding fresh slaves from the interior was proving harder as each week dragged by. Heavily armed patrols searched the jungle, but the natives were proving more and more elusive. As a stopgap, he had ordered the prisons emptied. The thieves and cut-throat wretches they contained were sent to labour in the mines. To his dismay, he had even been forced to dispatch ships to the West

Indies to procure black slaves, who arrived there occasionally from Africa, manacled and packed like animals in the dark stinking holds of slave ships. He clicked his tongue with irritation. Don Rodrigo knew he would have to pay a premium for them, to successfully outbid the local plantation owners, who, from time to time visited the slave markets to refresh their own depleted, diseased and overworked labour force.

Don Rodrigo's contemplation was interrupted suddenly, by a loud rap on the door. His servant, Fernandez, burst into the room unbidden, shattering his train of thought completely.

Angrily, the Governor leapt to his feet, and spluttered,

'What is the meaning of this, Fernandez?'

The white-haired servant bowed respectfully. He said nervously,

'Please forgive my intrusion, Excellency, but word has come that the crew of the Santa Juliana has just arrived.'

Don Rodrigo hammered his fist into his open palm with relief. At last, he thought, some good news. The tide was definitely beginning to turn in his favour. Forgetting his irritation at being disturbed, a thin smile cracked the usual sour look on his face. He gasped with relief, and enquired expectantly,

'The ship is safe then?'

His elation evaporated as quickly as it had risen when stone faced, the retainer shook his head,

'No Excellence. The report said that the Juliana was pursued and attacked by English pirates yesterday, and the crew was put ashore after the Juliana was captured.'

Grinding his teeth with frustration, the Governor slumped back into his leather-bound chair. On top of all his other woes, now he was assailed by pirates. Could anything, he wondered, possibly make his current situation any worse? His mind once again flashed back momentarily to the execution he had presided over, and the look in the Shaman's eyes, as he brought down his heathen curse.

Trying his best to put the thought from his mind; breathing deeply to control his surging anger, Don Rodrigo slowly placed his palms over his thin face, leant forward and snapped,

'Have the Juliana's captain brought before me immediately. Summon Colonel Alveraz and Admiral Ramos. Warn them that I want an emergency meeting to deal with the new threat of pirates. Show them in, as soon as I have finished with the damned coward who lost me a fortune in silver.

Fernandez bowed low, momentarily relieved he had gone into service, and not followed a military career. Respectfully, he bowed again and said, 'As you command, Excellency.'

* * *

Richard and Quinn crept forward, quickly crossed the clearing and followed the dark-skinned men into the jungle's dense undergrowth. Richard joined the narrow trail they had used to make their disappearance. Both he and Quinn strained to hear any noise ahead, but they heard nothing except ever-present birdsong and the occasional cry of a distant animal. With visibility on the jungle floor down to little more than a few yards in places, Richard was concerned they might suddenly blunder into another clearing, and be seen by the men they were intent on pursuing. Worse still, they might literally stumble upon the hunting party, as they rested. Richard knew he had no choice but push on. The strangers were too close to the bay where the Hawk and Juliana lay, to simply ignore their threat.

Both men made good progress, but slowed again when the jungle undergrowth became thicker. Quinn eyed the green surroundings with trepidation. He didn't like the idea that an army of savages could be hidden within bowshot range. He had heard rumours in the smoky bars which surrounded Plymouth harbour, from men who had recently returned from the New World, that the natives who lived in the jungle took the heads of their enemies after killing them, and through some dark and devilish process, shrunk their grisly trophies down to the size of a man's fist. Quinn swallowed, as he absently ran his broad hand around his neck. He for one had no desire to become an ornament on some dark-skinned savage's belt.

As the two men slowed their pace, the jungle seemed to close in around them, until the path on which they trod seemed to simply fade away to nothing. Richard raised his hand. Quinn saw the signal and stopped behind his master. Richard stared at his servant, and whispered,

'It's no good, Quinn…we've lost them…'

Before Quinn could reply, somewhere close, behind the wall of green foliage, with the sound of a pistol shot, a branch suddenly snapped. Startled by the loud crack, both Quinn and Richard spun abruptly towards the noise. Standing just a few yards away, a tall black man had appeared ghost-like from behind the moss covered trunk of a tree. In his hands, were two pieces of freshly broken stick.

Both Englishmen's hands flew towards their sword handles. Shaking his coal-black head, the tall negro dropped the pieces of wood and clapped his hands together. Surrounding them, dark figures appeared from the undergrowth, each of them holding a drawn bow. Razor-sharp flint arrowheads pointed at Quinn and Richard's heaving chests.

In broken, heavily accented Spanish, the tall negro said,

'You prisoners…move, and you dead!'

Chapter Twelve

Don Rodrigo scowled as he listened to the sweating master of the Juliana, who stood nervously before the Governor and made his report. Head bowed and holding his wide-brimmed hat in trembling hands; Captain Sanchez spoke falteringly, and did his best to deflect criticism and explain why he had managed to remain alive after losing a hold full of silver bars.

'The English pirate fell upon us without warning, your Excellence. He appeared out of the morning mist like a ghost, pretending to be one of my own flotilla. Our ships had been split up by the tempest; you see. The Juliana became separated, through no-one's fault, in the great storm which raged throughout the previous night. I have never seen such waves, and the wind threatened to snap the masts; it was so strong. It was necessary to run before the storm, that's why our flotilla broke formation. In the madness of the wind, it was every ship for itself.'

The Governor eyed the Captain coldly. 'Go on,' he hissed through clenched teeth.

Captain Sanchez swallowed. His mouth was dry, but to his dismay, the laws of hospitality had been ignored since he had entered the private office. Ominously, he was offered no refreshments, despite a well-stocked table to one side of the Governor's desk. The captain tugged at his collar.

It had been a long, gruelling walk along the deserted beach line. Unarmed and fearing at any moment an attack by natives, they had been forced to walk without proper rest, by day and night, until he and his crew had eventually reached the safety of Veracruz. His tongue felt swollen and thick. The Captain was thirsty, and felt utterly exhausted.

'Please, your Excellence, may I have a drink of water before I continue?'

99

Don Rodrigo eyed the dishevelled sailor with barely concealed contempt. The man's clothes were certainly creased and dusty. His face was streaked with sweat and grime, but there were no signs of ripped garments or physical injury. The Governor had received a brief report from his guard commander, before the captain was admitted. The officer had told him that none of the crew showed signs of battle; with a grin, he added; just blisters on their feet.

The Governor laced his fingers together, and stared at Sanchez. The man showed no outward sign of putting up a fight. He said coldly, 'Water is for heroes, Captain. Finish your report, and then we'll see to your needs…' Abruptly he snapped, 'Now get on with it!'

Sanchez nodded. He knew, as master of the Juliana, responsibility for the loss of his ship, and its valuable cargo rested squarely on his shoulders. Things appeared to be going badly for him. He must choose his next words very carefully.

'The English pirate ship was fast, Excellence. It chased us for hours, but we couldn't shake him. He was like a man possessed, their captain. I had loaded my guns, and we, aboard the Juliana were ready to fight to the death of course. When they were close, their captain gave absolutely no warning that he was about to attack. He turned sharply in a most cowardly and dishonourable fashion, and ignoring the rules of war, opened fire on my stern, killing several of my men.' Sanchez spread his hands, and continued. 'I immediately returned fire of course with my stern gun, and as it became obvious later, managed to do considerable damage to the pirate's bow.'

Don Rodrigo nodded, as Sanchez warmed to the role of hero.

'When the English shattered my rudder and mizzen with their broadside, it left us helpless in the water. I could not manoeuvre, or make good my escape. We had to wait helplessly while the English pirates came alongside and grappled with us.'

100

To reinforce the hopelessness of their position on the high seas, Sanchez sighed deeply. 'We were heavily outnumbered, and the English were armed to the teeth, while as a merchant vessel, we had only a few old cannon, muskets and knives to beat off a very determined attack.' The captain sighed again, and shook his head sadly, 'We fired our main guns too of course, but we are civilian sailors, unskilled in the ways of war. Reloading was impossible, you know how difficult that is to accomplish on a calm day, let alone when under fire.'

The Spaniard was right on that matter at least, and both men knew it. Unlike the English ships, who withdrew their guns back inside the hull using blocks and pulleys to facilitate quick reloading, Spanish cannon were not mounted on wheeled carriages. One of the gun crew had to shimmy, unprotected and alone, along the hot barrel outside, and ram powder, wadding and ball, while remaining balanced precariously above the open water below.

'When they boarded us, the pirates were clearly lusting after our blood. As soon as the first of them put a foot on our deck, they immediately began killing helpless, unarmed men.' Sanchez let out a shudder as he reinforced his version of the capture of the Juliana. 'I could not permit this…In that one terrible moment; I saw it, as the Saints are my witness. It was my sacred duty to try and protect my crew from what would have been a most terrible and senseless slaughter. I had to save at least some of his majesty's brave and most valiant sailors; at the hands of those vile, murdering English.' Captain Sanchez lifted his head slowly. From somewhere, despite his thirst, he had managed to conjure a tear, which rolled down through the grime on his sweat streaked cheek, 'And so Excellence,' he added passionately, 'to avoid needless loss of life; faced with an utterly hopeless situation; I had no alternative but to surrender my ship to the English scum who had hunted us down and attacked us without mercy.'

101

Don Rodrigo nodded and sat in silence for a moment, while he considered the captain's story. The scowl on his face appeared to dissolve as he enquired,

'You say you did cause damage to the English ship, Captain?' Sanchez' face brightened slightly, as he noticed the Governor's stern face relax.

'Yes, Excellence! Some of my men were forced to help bail out a forward locker room, where one of my shots had put a good sized hole in the pirate ship. The English were very concerned about the amount of damage I had inflicted on them. Their captain feared they would sink, and ordered temporary repair to keep her seaworthy. I knew nothing of this, until on our march back to Veracruz, one of my own carpenters, who had helped with the bailing, told me of the temporary repairs the English had made. In his opinion, they certainly wouldn't hold for very long in rough seas, and they would have no alternative but to beach their ship, to repair it properly.'

Rodrigo's eyes narrowed, as he listened, then abruptly held up his hand,

'You are sure about that, Captain? The English ship was badly damaged by the bow?'

Captain Sanchez nodded enthusiastically,

'Yes...yes Excellence! They put us ashore as they made arrangements to tow the Juliana away, to make repair to both ships.'

Don Rodrigo sat back in his chair. His mind whirled with the possibilities for advancement, which had suddenly fallen before him. If the English ship was as badly damaged as the Juliana's captain was suggesting, and the Spanish ship was also temporarily crippled, there was every chance that both ships might be discovered beached, and be recaptured. If that was the case, there was the tantalising reek of reward everywhere. Don Rodrigo's heart began to pound, as his mind churned with possibilities.

If his men were vigilant, the Juliana's precious cargo could still be returned to him, and a valuable English frigate would be his. At least some of the English crew, if they could be taken alive, could be sent back in chains to the King in Madrid. A gift like that was almost beyond measure. It would make the name of Torrez spoken with admiration and respect. Past memories would quickly fade, at the lack of glory after the debacle on the poisoned island of Malta. Politically, it would send shockwaves all the way to the heretic English Queen's palace. King Phillip would reward him most generously, even as he handed the captured pirates over to meet their fate in his deepest dungeons, at the skilled hands of the dreaded Inquisition.

The next treasure laden convoy was not due to sail for Spain for at least another two weeks. Don Rodrigo sat back and considered his options carefully. Until they set sail as escorts to the wallowing convoy of galleons, he had eight heavily armed warships at his disposal to hunt down the Englishmen.

He was almost finished with the master of the Juliana. The story of the merchantman's capture might not stand up to closer scrutiny, he decided, but for now Don Rodrigo was satisfied that there could not have been any other outcome, no matter how Sanchez had embellished the truth, or sought to mitigate his own cowardice and surrender.

Don Rodrigo turned his attention back towards Sanchez. Suddenly standing up, he crossed to the side table, and filled a glass with cool sparkling water from a crystal carafe. He returned to his desk, sat down and pushed the glass towards the captain, who remained swaying and utterly drained before him.

'Here!' he snapped coldly, 'drink this man, before you fall down.'

It was not compassion which prompted the Governor's actions. One question remained unasked, and if all things went to the plan, which was rapidly coalescing in his mind, it could well be the most important question of all. A simple drink of water should revive Sanchez sufficiently to clear his mind, and get the answer the Don keenly sought.

Such men as Drake, Howard and Frobisher were well-known in the New World. Their attacks and plundering of peaceful Spanish shipping was a running sore on the honour of Spain. In the last few years, these devils had proved elusive; their crimes had gone unpunished for far too long. Unfolding before Don Rodrigo was a supreme opportunity to right the wrongs done by these foul English pirates, and rebuild Spain's damaged reputation as a naval power. Capture of just one of these men, the Don knew, would make his position unassailable in the eyes of his King, when Don Rodrigo eventually returned in triumph to Spain with his prisoners.

Safely in chains, any one of these infamous privateer captains could be handed over to the Inquisition, whose torturers would extract a signed confession that the captured pirate was secretly in the employ of the heretic English Queen. As a result of such an admission, the broken prisoner would be an international pawn of almost incalculable value to the Spanish Empire.

As victor in the New World, bravely fighting against the English piratical heretics, Don Rodrigo shuddered at the thought of his own personal glory in the eyes of both Crown and Church. A cruel smile played across his lips as he dreamt of giving evidence during the crushed privateer's show trial in Madrid, and the prisoner's public execution which would certainly follow.

His cold eyes suddenly glittering with anticipation, the Governor of Veracruz lent forward again and said,

'Now answer me, Sanchez... who exactly was it that took your ship? ...' The tension surrounding him was almost too much to bear. The Don's fist suddenly pounded the desktop,

'*Tell me his name!*'

104

Chapter Thirteen

'Don't resist or struggle, Quinn,' hissed Richard, as his hands were bound tightly behind his back by two of the hunters.

Eyes blazing, Quinn glared at his captors. The giant Cornishman rumbled, 'But I can still take them, master!'

Straining against his bonds, Richard shook his head. There were too many arrows pointed at them,

'No Quinn! For the love of Christ man, now is not the time... Don't resist...'

Quinn's eyes still blazed, but to Richard's relief, he saw his servant's shoulders suddenly slump, as he accepted this temporary defeat.

Once both men with tightly bound, the leader of the band nodded into the jungle. His men understood the gesture; Richard and Quinn were pushed back onto the trail, and led away...

* * *

'WHAT!'

The colour drained from his thin face. Don Rodrigo's eyes flashed momentarily with dumbfounded disbelief. His mouth suddenly felt bitter and dry; his breathing came in rapid gasps; white knuckled hands gripped the arm rests on his chair. Heart hammering inside his chest, in that moment, further words eluded him. The Governor of Veracruz sat frozen, staring at Sanchez with his mouth open as his mind whirled. Could this be true? Could his greatest enemy in all the world actually be here, hiding somewhere close by in the jungles of his province?

Fighting to recover a little of his earlier composure; head still shaking slowly with disbelief, Don Rodrigo snapped,

'Are you absolutely sure? He definitely said the name Starkey?... Sir.. Richard.. Starkey?

Sanchez nodded rapidly and spluttered,

'Yes, yes Excellence. There is no doubt in my mind. When the Juliana was taken, the English captain came aboard and introduced himself to me, and my officers... He was an English knight; he said his name was Richard Starkey... I am sure Excellence; yes, yes, I am absolutely positive!'

The Don's mind flashed back in time to the distant blood-soaked shores of Malta, and the loathing he had seen oozing from every pore of Starkey's face. Then, pure chance had denied Rodrigo the opportunity of killing his enemy, while he had him helpless. He had Starkey at his mercy, but with the untimely arrival of the Englishman's manservant, it was not to be. This time it would be very different; he thought. This time, his arch enemy was not protected by a well-positioned uncle, or a Grand Master who favoured the Englishman. Starkey was alone, and his ships were badly damaged. The Don's mind raced pell-mell; there was much to plan and arrange. He looked up. He was done with Sanchez for now,

'Very well, Captain. That is enough. See to your men, and take refreshment and rest. I will send for you again, if I require more information.' Don Rodrigo looked down at the papers before him. 'Now get out, and tell Colonel Alveraz and Admiral Ramos to attend me immediately.'

With an imperious sweep of his hand, Don Rodrigo dismissed the exhausted merchant captain from the chamber. Glad to be released from the threat of imminent arrest, and the scornful, piercing gaze of the Governor, Sanchez bowed obsequiously before backing away for several paces. Still kneading his wide-brimmed hat with sweating hands, he turned sharply. Wrenching one of the heavy wooden doors open, he gratefully fled the chamber, and made his escape.

Almost immediately, there was a loud rap on the door. It quickly swung open and Fernandez appeared. Clearing his throat, he announced them, as Colonel Alveraz and Admiral Ramos strode past the secretary into the chamber. The contrast

106

between the two officers was marked. Alveraz was tall, lean and upright; he carried himself with the haughty bearing of the professional soldier he was. Ramos, however, was quite the opposite. He was short, ruddy-faced and distinctly chubby. His liking for port had given him a pronounced limp, which he supported with a cane. The gout, always sore and sometimes cruelly painful, had come on over the years. It bothered his left knee and ankle, and was now made immeasurably worse by the hot and unforgiving climate of the New World.

As both men stopped short of the Governor's desk and bowed their salute, Ramos extracted a lace handkerchief from his pocket, and mopped his sweating brow.

'By all the Saints, damn this heat!' he muttered to himself under his breath. He winced at the surge of pain in his leg as he straightened. The Governor ignored his discomfort.

'Gentlemen, please be seated.' Don Rodrigo swept a hand towards the two chairs on one side of his desk. Admiral Ramos let out an audible sigh of relief as he sat down. The chair creaked in protest as it took the strain of his excessive weight.

The Governor dispensed with the niceties, and came straight to the point. Keeping his private agenda to himself, he announced grandly,

'It has come to my attention that the English pirate, Sir Richard Starkey, a contemporary of Drake and Howard, and known favourite of his blasphemous Queen, is hunting the seas of the New World; somewhere close to Veracruz.' The Governor paused for a moment, and then continued, 'My intelligence suggests he is responsible for the capture of the Santa Juliana. However, both ships are crippled, and currently beached.' A conspiratorial smile crept across his face, 'With you searching the land, Alveraz, and you the sea, Ramos, we have been blessed, should we capture him, with a wonderful opportunity for advancement, glory and I would imagine, substantial reward from our grateful and beloved King...'

107

Both Richard and Quinn were sweating freely, as they matched the fast pace of the hunting party. Clearly acclimatised to the humidity and heat of the jungle, their barefooted captors showed no sign of distress as they plunged through the undergrowth on a hidden path towards their ultimate destination. No words were spoken; their coal-black scout used only hand signals, which the other men obviously understood, and reacted to, instantly.

Richard watched the men in front of him closely. These were certainly not local natives; they were of mixed races and seemed more like well-trained irregulars, or perhaps even a localized militia. Richard cursed to himself. These men must be bounty hunters in the employ of the Spanish, and would bring their leader a handsome reward, when he and Quinn were handed over. Richard knew he had damned himself, for his rashness in following them from the waterhole. He realised he and Quinn's position was hopeless. The rest of his crew were busy in the lagoon, hard at work making repairs to the Hawk and Juliana. His hunting party would be following his orders; still patiently lying in ambush, waiting around the waterhole, oblivious to the fact that their Captain had been taken prisoner.

His men would be unaware of their Captain's disappearance until they failed to return to the ships at nightfall. William Howard, if he had any sense, would not raise a search party until dawn. Due to the dense canopy above, the jungle floor was pitch-black at night. Given the immensity of the jungle, and a burning torch's spill of light illuminating just a few feet ahead, it would be nothing short of madness to risk searching the darkness. It would also place the rescue party in dire peril of becoming hopelessly lost in the dark jungle's depths.

With no hope of immediate rescue, Richard decided that he and Quinn would just have to bide their time, and make a break for it, if and when an opportunity presented.

Richard's train of thought was interrupted abruptly, when the leader of the group suddenly raised his hand. The hunting party stopped and pulled down their captives; they crouched quickly around their prisoners and while the nearest held his finger to his lips, the others froze. Their leader remained standing and cupped his hands together, making a high-pitched bird-cry. It was answered in similar fashion from somewhere close ahead; neither Richard nor Quinn could see the creature which made it, until a small man appeared from the curtain of jungle just yards away, and urgently beckoned the party forward.

The men around Richard smiled and visibly relaxed. They stood up and hauled both captives to their feet. Richard and Quinn were pushed through the jungle's curtain into a clearing. Ahead of them, a collection of bamboo walled huts, thatched with broad palm leaves appeared, built above ground on stilt-like legs. A score of black and fair-skinned women, huddled around various cooking fires, looked up in surprise and paused from their duties. Curiosity aroused; children around them stopped playing and also stared intently at the new faces thrust into their midst. Alerted to their arrival, a handful of young and old men, some carrying homemade spears and bows also appeared.

Like Richard, Quinn was equally shocked at the unexpected and sudden advent of both the settlement and its rag-tag population. The party's leader motioned them towards the centre of the huts, and called out a name, in a hard, guttural accent which sounded strangely familiar to Richard.

'Hey... *Hendrik!*

Moments later, throwing the rattan curtain aside, a gaunt man appeared from the nearest hut. He was clearly of European origin, despite his skin burnt to the colour of tanned leather by the unrelenting sun. He was bearded, with one piercing blue eye. The other side of his face was rent by a long jagged scar which sliced deeply across a dark and empty eye socket. His matted hair hung down and rested across narrow shoulders. Like the others

109

in the settlement, the man was barefoot; his beard and the clothing he wore gave him the air of a castaway, Richard thought; it was threadbare and heavily patched.

The man stared at the two prisoners for a moment, unable to hide his surprise. Intrigued, he stepped forward onto the slatted platform immediately in front of the open doorway. Without breaking stride, he descended the rough wooden steps to the compacted ground below.

In hushed tones, the hunting party captain explained to the man, who Richard assumed was his leader, what had transpired, and why two strangers now stood tightly bound before him.

While they talked together, Richard's eyes swept the settlement for clues, seeking an answer to this strange puzzle. He could see the inhabitants were a mixture of age and races, and all appeared thin but healthy. There was no sign of leprous sores or contagion on any of them, however. Unbidden, dark memories of the isolated Priory of St. Lazarus leper colony, built on the rugged coastline of northern Malta, flooded Richard's memory. He suppressed a shuddered and quickly dismissed the haunting images that he remembered of the walking dead. As his captors conversed, Richard's eyes continued to sweep the crude village. To his relief, there was no sign of uniformed soldiers or hooded priests, which was certainly odd, in any outpost controlled by the Spanish Crown, no matter how remote. There was no evidence of iron tools, or modern weapons either. This was a village, Richard thought, on the very edge of civilisation. He frowned. It made no sense at all; these people were not locals, and this was no native settlement. In Richard's mind, there was something distinctly odd going on here. The settlement was too far from the sea for its inhabitants to be common pirates.

Suddenly, the gaunt European nodded, muttered something and stepped forward towards the captives. He stood before Quinn, turned his head and muttered something over his shoulder to the others in the hunting party. There was a swirl of

110

laughter from the men, which made Quinn rumble dangerously. Straining against his bonds, he scowled back towards his captors. The laughter faded quickly as their leader turned his attention to Richard. This prisoner's buckled shoes and well-cut clothing suggested a higher social station than that of the giant standing beside him. Placing his legs apart and his hands on his hips, the jungle chief inquisitively canted his head to one side and enquired in passable Spanish,

'Before my men take you away and kill you, admit it, you Spanish bastards, you are spies come from the ships in the lagoon. Are your orders to reconnoitre, and then bring soldiers here to recapture us?'

Richard stared at his captor for a moment. His heart began to pound as realisation of the truth coursed through him – 'recapture us' - *Of course!*

In his own native tongue, Richard answered slowly,

'Yes, we are from the lagoon, but we are Englishmen, not Spaniards.' To reinforce the point he quickly added, 'and sworn enemies of King Phillip of Spain.' Richard paused for a moment, as shock registered on his captor's scarred face, 'Perhaps I am wrong,' he added hastily, 'but I believe you and your people don't exactly cleave to the Spanish Crown either, do you?'

The chieftain's good eye suddenly darkened. Like a dam bursting to the pressure of the sea, he spat out his answer, which was filled with a tidal wave of bitterness and loathing,

'We are no friends to that prancing Catholic despot, or his cruel, swaggering Conquistadors!'

Richard nodded. He thought so. This was a critical juncture. To avoid further offence at such a delicate moment, he softened his voice as he said apologetically,

'Forgive me,' Richard shrugged, 'but if my enemy's enemy is my friend, then it seems, against all the odds, we are met here as allies... Judging by you accent; like us, you are a long way from home?' When no reply came, Richard pressed on, 'Tell me, if I

111

have guessed correctly, what is a Hollander doing here, living hidden in the depths of this wild Godless jungle?...I believe I know the answer. You are escaped slaves, are you not?'

The look of shock flashed again across the chieftain's face. The exchange might just buy them enough time to fully explain their presence, before Richard and Quinn were taken back into the jungle and had their throats cut. It seemed to Richard that he saw traces of something akin to a flash of hope behind the man's expression. Something about him made Richard believe that he looked as though he wanted to accept their story, but his good eye appeared hooded with suspicion and his words remained edged with doubt. Warily he slipped into accented English.

'You… you are not Spaniards, then?'

Richard shook his head and smiled reassuringly.

'No! Absolutely not! We are both free-born Englishmen.' Half turning, he added. 'This huge rascal beside me is my manservant, who answers to the name of Quinn.'

The leader of the escaped slaves nodded. He turned his gaze away from Quinn's bulk, back to Richard,

'If you are not Spanish spies, then who, exactly, are you?'

Richard took a deep breath and ignoring his bonds, made a half step backwards and inclined his head forward. As he quickly straightened, he said,

'Permit me to introduce myself. I am Sir Richard Starkey; loyal subject of Queen Elizabeth of England, and Privateer Captain of the frigate, Sea Hawk,' with an ironic smile playing across his lips, he raised an eyebrow and added, 'and I'm also the new owner of the Spanish galleon, the Santa Juliana.' Defiantly, he added 'God bless and save her majesty!'

Beside him, Quinn scowled again at his captors. Mirroring his master's defiance, he drew himself up and rumbled through gritted teeth,

'Aye…you heathen bastards, God save the Queen!'

112

There was a moment of uneasy silence between captor and captives. Richard turned and frowned at his servant. He whispered softly,

'Easy Quinn... I believe we just might be among friends.'

The Dutchman heard the whisper as he stared intently from one captive to the other. He saw no subterfuge or deception in their faces; there was nothing but truth in the steely, honest English eyes which returned his gaze.

After many months of keeping his rag-tag community alive in the jungle wilderness, once again, the Dutchman was faced with the heavy burden of making a decision which could affect his people's survival. If he chose badly, their crude but dignified existence as free men and women would end at the hands of the hated Spanish. However, if he was ever to escape the bonds of the jungle and see the crowded wharfs of Amsterdam again, the Dutchman would have to trust his instincts and believe the tale told by these two strangers. There was only one way to be sure these men were not King Phillip's spies. He must gamble his own life, in his own way. He knew that was the only way to be absolutely certain.

With a sigh, his mind made up; he turned to one of his men and snapped,

'*Release them!*'

Chapter Fourteen

Richard sat beside one of the cooking fires. A leg of the freshly butchered boar was being turned on a spit by a small boy, as he roasted it slowly over a bed of bright flames. Hot fat dripped from the meat, sizzling and smoking as it dripped onto the glowing coals beneath it. Besides Richard, his hungry manservant sat with his eyes glued to the roasting pork. Quinn smacked his lips as his nose wrinkled with delight at the wonderful aroma which enveloped him. It would be the first decent meat he had tasted in more than six long months. Still raptly focused on the treat before him, his nostrils flared and quivering, Quinn muttered,

'Almost too much to bear, this is, Master …Waiting, I mean.'

Richard half-smiled at his manservant's impatience and turned to Hendrik, who had just sat down and joined them.

'So how did you come to be here, Hendrik?' Richard enquired.

The Dutchman scratched his bearded chin and shrugged. With a sigh, he began his tale,

'I was taken one night by the Spanish from my home in Amsterdam. My arrest was ordered by that bloody bastard the Duke of Alva. Without explanation or just cause, he imprisoned me in a stinking military jail.' He snorted, 'all in the name of the Catholic Church and the King of Spain.' His hand crept involuntarily towards his scarred face, 'They put out my eye with a hot iron while they tortured me for information; the names of men they alleged were my co-conspirators. I gave away nothing, for I knew nothing. Eventually, they gave up on me. It didn't matter though; while I remained chained in my cell, I was tried in my absence for crimes I didn't commit. The Court of the Inquisition found me guilty, naturally. My sentence was to have

114

my ships and business confiscated, but they hadn't finished with me though,' he added bitterly. 'Alva's soldiers turned my family out of our home and seized it. They didn't want to make a martyr of me, or soil their dainty hands with my blood, so I was moved from the prison late one night. They chained me in the hold of one of their ships, and transported me, along with many others like me to this stinking hellhole; to work in the mines until we died.' Hendrik hung his head with the heavy burden of dredging up his darkest memories.

Richard nodded. He had heard rumours of Spanish behaviour towards the subjugated Dutch before. This poor fellow had lost everything. Richard asked gently, 'What happened to your family?'

Hendrik shook his head sadly. The lank hair which had fallen across his face hid his expression, but Richard could hear despair and grief in the man's voice.

'I don't know. I wasn't allowed to communicate with the outside world during my imprisonment, and only knew that my wife and children had been evicted from our home, when the guard captain read out the court's sentence, through the bars of my cell.'

The Hawk's master frowned.

'But what was your crime? If you were innocent, why did they take you, and treat you so harshly?' Richard's tone betrayed his confusion.

Hendrik snorted, and spat his next words out,

'My crimes?' He was silent for a moment, and then he continued, 'I was rich and prosperous. I owned one of the biggest trading companies in Amsterdam. My ships travelled across the seas to the furthest ports in the known world in search of trade and spices, but you see; my family are Calvinists, and we are hated above all others by the Spanish, and their vile running-dogs of the Catholic Church.'

Richard nodded. Hendrik's words confirmed the oppression and religious persecution metered out to the opponents of the Spanish King; by the priests of his dreaded Inquisition. Phillip's tyranny had caused many Dutch families to flee across the cold waters of the English Channel. There were thousands of Huguenot and Calvinist exiles in England. His Queen had granted them asylum. As fellow Protestants, considered enemies of the Holy See in Rome, she defied Spain and the Catholic Church. Elizabeth made certain the refugees were made welcome within her realm.

His heart heavy, Hendrik continued bitterly with his story.

'Even before my arrest, we were forced to worship in secret while the Spanish openly looted and burnt our churches. We were denounced as heretics, and declared enemies of God, and of the state.'

Richard stared at his former captor. He guessed wildly,

'So what did you do, burn down one of their churches?'

Hendrik looked up. The hair fell away; his anguish became clear,

'No, I didn't personally, but alas; it was one of the hotheads among my men who did. He was betrayed and arrested, but the Spanish military handed their prisoner over to the Bishop of Amsterdam and his wicked priests of the Inquisition. It was deemed to have become an ecclesiastical matter, you see? Those bastard priests claimed jurisdiction over the incident. They said their filthy holy relics were destroyed, and sanctified ground had been defiled by Satan worshiping, Calvinist rebels.'

Richard winced and nodded, The Catholic Bishop responsible for his flock in Amsterdam must have been furious with a direct attack on his church,

'So what happened?' he whispered.

Hendrik looked up sharply. 'Alva and Bishop of Amsterdam jointly decreed it had been a gross act of religious

116

desecration. Making a public example of a mere low born was not enough for them, so they arranged to implement and blame me, as owner and head of the de Wit Trading Company. Their key was the prisoner they held, you see. He was employed as one of my stevedores, and had been caught hiding in one of my warehouses down on the waterfront, in the Durgerdam district…The Inquisition made sure my name was prominent in the man's confession…' Hendrik exhaled slowly. 'Their torturer priests made short work of him… Oh; he signed it all right. By the time they had finished with him, the poor devil would have signed anything.' Hendrik shrugged fatalistically. 'And that was that. Under Spanish law I was now a convicted criminal and they had the legal right to confiscate my business and fortune, and divide it up between the Church, Alva and the Spanish Crown.'

Richard's jaw dropped as he seethed at the terrible injustice,

'But… but that's simply outrageous, Hendrik!

Hendrik shrugged with resignation as he stared bitterly into the glowing coals of the campfire,

'You must remember, Sir Richard, unlike England, my people live under the yoke of oppression in the Netherlands. You have no idea…The Spanish do as they please within their conquered dominions. With Alva's powerful, heavily armed army of occupation, who or what could stop them?'

Richard knew Hendrik was right, but the wickedness and cruelty heaped upon the Protestant people of Holland bit deeply; it wounded Richard's sense of natural justice. What also fanned the flames of concern in his mind, however, was something he remembered from months ago. Before he set sail for the New World, a secret was revealed to him during his last audience with the Queen, which had made his blood run cold. Richard had been advised of the covert intelligence that Walsingham had gathered from his agents in Spain. He was informed of the

117

Spaniards advanced preparations to invade England, and the great Armada which was under construction.

Hendrik looked up and stared across the scattered huts of the small settlement. 'Most of the people here have similar stories to tell,' he said wearily. 'They have been torn from their homes and families by the Spanish, and used here, as slaves.'

Richard nodded, 'You said most of the people?'

'We have a few genuine escaped criminals among us as well,' a thin smile crept over Hendrik's tortured face as he shrugged, 'who are as guilty as sin. To be transported here to the mines was also their punishment, but we are all redeemed in the eyes of God and made equal again, after escaping from the Spanish, and our cruel lives of bondage…'

Hendrik's story was a bitter one, filled with pain and sorrow. Richard feared it would be repeated many times over, in the leafy shires of his own country, if the Spanish Armada ever made it safely to England's gentle shores.

In that moment, Walsingham's distant briefing, and Hendrik's tragic tale pulled everything together in Richard's worried mind. It all made complete and terrible sense. The riches stolen from his scattered dominions, and now the New World were filling King Phillip's coffers even faster than Walsingham suspected, and would soon pay for the conquest of England. Richard's expression hardened as his mind focused; his duty became clear. He held his Queen's Letter of Marque. Its Royal Seal gave him more than permission simply to loot and sink scattered Spanish ships. It also gave him authority to wage unfettered war on England's enemies. Richard knew he must do everything he could, to save his beloved country from the threat of invasion, and the religious tyranny that would surely follow.

The lad turning the spit stopped suddenly, looked up and announced the meat was ready. Quinn slapped his broad thigh

118

and whooped with delight. Richard turned back to Hendrik. His mind still churning, he said,

'We will share your hospitality, and are grateful for it, Hendrik. Then we must away back to my ship before it gets dark.' He stared out above the surrounding tangle of the jungle's dense foliage, 'Will you come with us, and be our guide? Your assistance will be invaluable, if I am to singe Phillip's beard and take the fight to our enemy's heart.'

Hendrik nodded solemnly. He would be risking his life, but to be absolutely sure these men were genuine enemies of Spain, he must go with them. At last, if he was right, there was now a chance to go home, find his family, join the resistance and fight against Spanish tyranny. He had nothing to lose but his life; it was a gamble worth taking. He said,

'My people hate the Spaniards, Sir Richard. We want revenge on the swine who have raped, tortured and murdered our loved ones. They must answer with their blood for destroying our lives, and bringing us to die in this miserable place, which God has certainly forgotten.'

Hendrik's expression softened. His tanned skin wrinkled, as he smiled for the first time. 'I'm sure, when I speak to the others, they will be happy to help you too, in any and every way they can. In the meantime, I would be delighted to join you in a reconnaissance against our mutual enemy.'

Richard returned the smile and relaxed a little. Now he had allies; he was sure he could come up with a plan to thwart their enemies. Before he worked out his strategy, however, he needed as much information and intelligence as he could gather. He said,

'Tell me something of what you have learned of the Spanish occupation and their operations here, Hendrik.'

Hendrik nodded; it was a simple enough story.

'When I was a slave, because of my knowledge and experience in shipping, the Spanish put me to work in the port where the treasure fleet assembles. Its surrounding town and harbour are commonly known as Boca Del Rio, which means *Mouth of the River*. It lies on the coast, a few miles from the provincial capital of Veracruz.'

Richard nodded. 'How many ships can anchor in Boca Del Rio, and what of the harbour defences?'

Hendrik's face creased, as he searched back into his memory; he tried to remember the details.

'The harbour is shallow on one side, but more than adequate to berth twenty galleons in the deep water on the other,' he stopped speaking, and rubbed his hand over the leathery skin of his face before continuing. 'A shore battery in a stone fortress protects the narrow entrance to the harbour, but there is also a gun emplacement on the tiny island called Isla de Sacrificios, which lies just a few hundred yards outside the harbour mouth. While I was working in Boca Del Rio, there was an outbreak of fever. The Spanish were short of labour. I was blessed by the hand of God, and not touched by the sickness, so one day I was sent over to the island in a boat with some other slaves. We were ordered to dig out the embrasures and help site the guns.'

'How many cannon were out there?'

Hendrik snorted. 'As I remember, at least four in the fortress shore battery; three more on the island.'

Richard nodded. 'And how big were the guns?'

The Dutchman winced at the memory,

'The barrels were fat and very heavy, and almost impossible to move from the shoreline to the bunkers we had built. The Spanish brought them over one at a time because of their great weight, and it took all of us more than half a day using block and tackle to drag them up the beach and site each of them on their carriages. As I remember, the barrels were broad and at least twice the length of a man; the muzzles where almost big enough to hide a man's head in.'

120

Richard nodded again. The Spanish guns sounded like fifteen or more probably twenty pounders. He was no expert however, so he turned to Quinn, who was busy with his dagger, slicing another tasty morsel of meat from the steaming leg bone.

'Twice the length of a man and the muzzle's almost big enough to hide a man's head in? What do you think, Quinn?'

The big Cornishman stopped sawing at the meat and thought for a moment, as he pondered the question,

'Sounds more like a twenty pounder, I would say, master. Maybe even twenty-five... big powerful bastards they are. Slow to load, but pack a mighty punch when they hit something. Accuracy falls away sharply if the target is far off, though,' he added reflectively.

Richard pursed his lips; this news was as important, as it was bad. Two interlocking batteries would create a deadly crossfire at the harbour mouth. Anything entering without permission would be caught in a lethal trap, and be blown to pieces.

Richard thought for a moment, there was something else which troubled him. Without accurate charts of the waters around Boca Del Rio, any plan he made in an attack from the sea was doomed to failure. If one or both of his ships hit a submerged reef during the action, they would be sitting ducks for the Spanish guns. Blind to the dangers, the hand of death beckoned the unwary. Worse still, capture and a terrible end, at the hands of the fanatical devils of the Inquisition, awaited him and his crew, if he got things wrong. He said,

'Clearly, the harbour, filled with Spanish ships at anchor, is the key to doing harm to our enemy, by stopping the flow of treasure to Spain.' He grinned wolfishly, 'they might have all the gold in the world stored in Veracruz, Hendrik, but without sufficient ships to transport it; the Atlantic Ocean becomes a vast and impassable moat.'

121

Hendrik's eyes flashed. The English knight was right. Eagerly, the Dutchman said,

'So we seal the harbour off, and bottle-up the entire Spanish flotilla?'

Richard thought for a moment,

'Hmm, something like that, perhaps? We will spy out the harbour at Boca Del Rio tomorrow, Hendrik, if you can arrange a boat.' Richard thoughtfully chewed on a piece of pork for a moment, and then he said.

'Tell me about the Spanish presence here, Hendrik. I know of Veracruz, but little else of the enemy's dispositions. This is something I need to give careful thought to, when I plan our action. I will need much more detailed information before I finalise anything.' Richard stared at his host. 'Tell me, Hendrik; where is the Spaniards' gold kept, before it is loaded aboard the flotilla?'

Hendrik frowned and shook his head,

'No, Sir Richard! Don't think of trying to steal even a single ducat from their horde. The Governor's treasury in Veracruz is closely guarded day and night by cavalry and a full company of heavily armed musketeers. It would be an impossible task to break in, and only disaster would come of any attempt to steal the treasure it contains.'

As Richard shrugged his acknowledgement at the futility of attempting to sack the treasury, Hendrik smiled and raised his hand. There was a hint of conspiracy in the Hollander's voice as he said,

'But perhaps there is another way to capture a fortune? A great mule-train will arrive in a few weeks, carrying tons of gold and silver from the mines in Peru. Its arrival is always timed to coincide with the fleet preparing to leave for Spain. Maybe we have an advantage? The mule-train is due pretty soon, perhaps, in as little as two weeks or so from now?'

Richard ears pricked up. He said,

122

'A mule-train you say? And you think we have an advantage…because…?'

His spirits rose at another opportunity to hit back at the Spaniards; Hendrik smiled again, and replied,

'Because for the last forty leagues, the Spanish can use only one narrow trail through the hills and jungle leading into Veracruz; it's an old Inca trail. Long ago, before the Spanish came, the Inca Indians in the interior used to trade with the fishermen's settlements on the coast. Native runners would also use it to pass urgent messages between their leaders.'

The smile faded from his lined face, 'We have often talked of raiding the mule-train in the past, but without decent weapons to attack, and ships to transport our booty away, we simply risk bringing the wrath of the Governor and his legion of iron-shirts down upon our heads.'

Richard felt his heart begin to race at this latest piece of intelligence. It triggered something, a vivid, searing flash through his mind. The rough outline of a daring plan had begun to form, even as the Dutchman spoke. If it proved feasible, he just might be able to disrupt the flow of gold to Spain for at least a year, while the Spaniards reorganised and replaced their fleet. If the other part of his scheme worked, there was a chance, however slim, that he might return to his homeland and present a fortune in Spanish gold and silver to his Queen. Richard smiled inwardly to himself. Two things were certain if he was successful. There was a chance to buy precious time and delay the completion of the great Armada under construction in the seaward ports of Spain, but equally important, his actions would help enormously to pay for new ships and cannon, which England so desperately needed to defend his island home against the coming invasion.

Richard nodded gratefully towards his host, and then, at last turned his attention to the thick slices of pork, which Quinn had laid out on a broad green leaf before him. As he lifted a piece to his mouth, he paused, turning his attention back towards his host, before biting into it. As Richard savoured the rich meat's delicious flavour, something else tickled at the back of his mind.

'As I need to take a good look at the harbour, Hendrik, is there any way you can get us there?'

The Dutchman nodded. 'We use native boats to fish these waters sometimes, Sir Richard. We don't usually go that close, but I know the Spanish ignore the local Indians who do fish near the harbour.' He shrugged. 'I'm sure it can be done.'

One question remained unanswered; it was long overdue to be asked. Richard said,

'When I was a boy, Hendrik, my father taught me many things. He once told me that to prevail in war, I should always know my enemy.' He paused, and then continued thoughtfully, 'During the recent action, when I captured the Santa Juliana, both my ship and the Spaniard were sorely damaged. As a result, desperate to save the ships, I mistakenly paid little heed to enquiring of my prisoners, as to the capabilities and indeed, the quality of their leader, the Governor of Veracruz. Tell me, Hendrik, who is he, and what do you know of him?'

There was silence for a moment, then contemptuously, Hendrik spat out a tough lump of gristle. It landed amidst the glowing coals of the fire; it sizzled and smoked angrily.

Glaring, Hendrik turned his good eye toward Richard, and said,

'That one?' Hendrik snorted derisively. 'He is truly the Devil incarnate, my friend. My duties at Boca Del Rio brought me into almost daily contact with him. That swine is a man possessed of the darkest of demons; a man driven purely by selfish and ruthless greed. He has shown not one whit of mercy, since he took over from Don Alphonso, who died last year of the fever... Mass executions and cruelty have become the new Governor's trademark, since the first foul day he arrived here.'

124

Hendrik picked up a stick as he spoke, stirring the burning coals. He covered the hissing gristle, raising a shower of sparks and a thin wisp of acrid smoke. Bitterly, he continued,

'He is the Butcher of Veracruz, Sir Richard; a bastard beyond measure... his name: - Don Rodrigo Torrez....'

For an instant, there was silence in the small clearing. Suddenly, eyes blazing, Richard leapt to his feet.

Quinn spat out the meat he was chewing, and jumped up beside his scowling master.

Startled, Hendrik and the other men standing near the fire stared open-mouthed at the Englishmen; their sun-burnt faces masked with surprise.

'Don Rodrigo Salvador Torrez?' Richard hissed breathlessly, his chest heaving.

Confused by his new allies' sudden and explosive reaction, Hendrik replied almost apologetically,

'Yes, that's him... Rodrigo Salvador Torrez... But I don't understand. What is the matter, Sir Richard? Do you know of him?'

Richard glared in silence at Hendrik as he fought to compose himself. The Dutchman saw murder lurking behind the Englishman's eyes. Vengeance suddenly hung thick and heavy in the air which surrounded them. It enveloped the small huddle of men, like a cold invisible shroud.

Face flushed, Richard's hand strayed to the pommel of his sword. Slowly, he replied through gritted teeth,

'Yes, Hendrik, I know your Butcher of Veracruz...and as God is my witness... I am sworn to kill him!'

Chapter Fifteen

The inky darkness of the jungle night would have swallowed them up, but for the route Hendrik had taken. As the sun threw its last vestiges of purple and orange across the darkening sky, guided by the Dutchman, Richard and Quinn reached the bay where the Hawk and Juliana lay safely at anchor. The men had exchanged few words during their journey through the jungle, each lost in their own thoughts as they made their way back to the ships.

Hendrik led the way, followed by Richard. Quinn lumbered along close behind them, his belly full, and his mind filled with concern for his master. The giant Cornishman had served Richard for some years now, and thought he knew all his master's moods, until that is, he had heard Don Rodrigo was somewhere near. The haunted look, now in Sir Richard's eyes reminded Quinn somehow of a hunting wolf. His master seemed sharp, focussed and intent on tracking and killing his prey. The few times he had spoken as they tramped along yet another animal trail, had been to urge Hendrik onward. The hidden wound of the broken heart his master carried would never mend, Quinn knew, until Sir Richard's avowed revenge was complete. Don Rodrigo must lay dead before him; healing could begin only then.

* * *

Beneath the cries of patrolling seagulls, surrounded by the sparkling waters of the Yucatan Peninsula, with difficulty, Richard pushed aside his vengeance, and thought carefully about the events after they had returned to the hidden cove.

The repairs on the two ships were proceeding well. Having made his inspection of the skeletal supports in the Hawk's bow,

126

the damage done by the Spanish cannonball was not going to take as long as the master carpenter had first feared. The split and damaged spa had narrowly avoided full replacement. It now stood fully repaired, with a series of forged iron bands wrapped tightly around it. The splintered hull planks, which were attached to the oak spa, were currently being replaced, and later today his crew would hammer new caulking into the narrow gaps between each of them. Finally, boiling pitch would seal the vessel, make it watertight, and fully seaworthy again.

He had made useful allies of Hendrik and his people. There were some experienced seamen amongst them, who were more than willing to leave their jungle prison and supplement Richard's overstretched crew. In return, Richard had offered free passage to England, to any seaman or escaped slave who desired it. Fearing the mighty ocean, with nothing to gain by returning, many refused, but some did accept the offer of a chance to return to civilization. Hendrik had set them to work, salting fish, and gathering food. Hunting parties were sent into the jungle, to capture, and cage wild boar and deer for the long voyage across the Atlantic.

Apart from the Spaniards, Richard had explained, time was their enemy. If they were to successfully deny use of the Spanish ships, and attack the mule-train, they must destroy the assembling convoy, well before the mules arrived with their treasure in Veracruz. The mule-train was vulnerable in the jungle, but would be lost to Richard and his crew forever, if it made it to the sanctuary of the heavily armed protection which surrounded the Governor's treasury.

Once the English privateers showed their hand, and the port of Boca Del Rio was attacked, both Richard and Hendrik knew every Spaniard in the New World would be warned of their presence, and would begin searching for them, but if Richard could later fill his holds with Spanish gold and silver, their mission would be at an end, and it would be time to beat a hasty retreat, return to England, and claim the glory which would surely be his.

Richard smiled to himself as he considered the tiny craft he was now commanding, comparing it to the size and majesty of his frigate.

Hued from a single tree trunk felled from the jungle forest, the large fishing canoe was perfect for navigating the inshore currents and barely concealed blues and greens of the stony reefs, which slid silently below in the crystal-clear water. It proved an uncomfortable craft for those unused to the confines of its narrow hull. Stabilised by a narrow outrigger, the craft gained in speed, what it lacked in comfort. Its four occupants shifted uncomfortably from time to time during the canoe's passage. They all felt stiff and cramped after almost two hours of uneventful sailing along the calm, inshore waters.

The lateen sail, fixed to the canoe's short mast, billowed with the offshore breeze, as it propelled the small fishing boat smoothly through the water, it's barely visible wake faded quickly behind it, little more than one hundred yards from the rocks which had now become the coastline. A heaped fishing net, one side bordered with small slabs of natural cork lined the bottom of the skiff; beneath it were concealed weapons and mapmaking ink, quills and parchment.

Each of the boat's crew wore a battered wide-brimmed straw hat, woven from strips of dried jungle palm leaves. They provided excellent shade from the burning sun, which still beat down relentlessly, even though the sun only hung halfway to its zenith, after beginning its slow accent from the horizon, hours earlier. Shadows which fell across weathered faces added to the deception; exposed limbs were blackened; smeared with burnt ash to make them appear, from a distance anyway, to be nothing more than the native fishermen the canoe's crew pretended to be.

128

Richard's darkened arm rested on the crude tiller. He lay back, appearing outwardly relaxed, but in reality, he was intent on keeping the boat well away from the crashing Atlantic breakers, which continuously pounded the rocky shoreline. He was determined to avoid any chance mishap, or discovery by some sharp-eyed Spaniard gunner or sentry, as the rebel boat drew nearer to the port.

As they rounded a small peninsular, the wide entrance to the natural harbour hove into view. A crowded lattice of tall ship's masts and rigging appeared; masts and spas grew like a naked winter forest on one side the horseshoe cove of the harbour. To Richard's relief, the ships were anchored in rows tight together, against what appeared to be a long wooden wharf, which stretched to the beach. No doubt, he thought; it made the ships easier to load and guard. Richard smiled to himself. That would be of great help, for what he had in mind.

There was silence aboard the skiff; Richard could feel the tension growing among his tiny crew.

'Steady lads, we're nearly there,' he said reassuringly, 'We'll sweep through the sound between harbour and Isla de Sacrificios, then sail back in a wide loop, as if we are searching for a shoal of fish. We'll stay offshore while Hendrik casts the net, and Master Godshaw marks out the locations of the gun batteries and records a safe, deep-water route for us, into the harbour.'

'Will you be sounding the depth, Captain?' Humble Godshaw enquired.

Richard nodded,

'Aye, we must find a clear channel, and mark any hazard beneath the water which might endanger our mission. To fool any sentry that might be observing us, I'll do my best to mask dropping the weight over the side, and then read off the measurements to you, as you mark the water's depth, relative to our position on your chart.'

'What shall I do, Master?' Quinn enquired.

'If the wind drops away, I'll need all your strength to help paddle us out of trouble, Quinn' Richard nodded his head towards the harbour mouth, 'I don't know if they have a naval picket boat patrolling the harbour, but if we see one, we can't risk them catching up with us. You are our lookout. If you spy anything other than small fishing boats, warn me instantly. I don't want to let any curious Spaniard get too close to us.'

Pleased with such responsibility, Quinn lent forward and picked up a broad, flat bladed paddle which was lodged between his feet. He hefted its weight, and then dipped it into the water for a moment. Satisfied, Quinn lifted the wet blade clear and rested it across his knees.

Rumbling, 'Ready Master,' Quinn proudly began his watch, staring intently at the harbour mouth and the little island opposite, through the narrowed slits of his eyes.

* * *

As the sentries patrolled their perimeter back at the cove, the repairs on the two ships continued. Under the stern gaze of the officers, and the watchful eyes of the carpenters' mates, hammers rang and sparked against crude iron nails as the Juliana's new rudder began to take form. Heavy wooden cross-pieces where being firmly attached to the tall blade of the rudder, before it was declared finished by the master carpenter, and heaved with rope and pulley, by lines of sweating crewmen. When it was finally swung into place and hung upright at last, the ship's carpenters would firmly attach it to the Juliana's repaired stern.

On the jetty, at the prow of the Hawk, the air was filled with the acrid smell of smoking braziers and cauldrons of bubbling pitch. All was being made ready, as the first line of caulking was pounded into place by a gang of sweating sailors.

130

The fresh meat Richard's hunting party had brought back the previous afternoon, supplemented by fish caught in the river had provided a feast for the Hawk's crew after the sun had gone down, and the preceding day's work was at an end. Armed with knowledge, garnered from many years at sea, and knowing the discomfort of living under harsh discipline and cramped conditions, Quinn's idea had worked. Fresh, decent meat and full bellies had lifted the seamen's morale from the almost mutinous depths it had sunk into.

Not everyone aboard the Hawk was happy and content, however. Irish Jack threw down the long iron ladle he had been stirring the molten pitch with, and cursed loudly, as a tiny splash of the bubbling liquid landed on his naked foot, for the third time that morning.

'Damn this!' he seethed, as he hopped across the wooden jetty nursing his rapidly blistering foot. 'Why do I get the worst job, eh? I know who is behind this. He's got it in for me, that Cornish bastard!' The others around him kept their heads down, lest he see the smirks and sniggers spreading across their sun-burnt faces. He was right, of course, and they all knew it.

'Serves the bugger right,' one sailor whispered to his mate who was working close beside him. His friend grunted his agreement. Stirring the spitting cauldron was well-known among experienced seamen. It was the worse job on the dock, and Irish Jack knew who had made sure he got the onerous task.

'I'll make that big red headed bugger pay for this,' he muttered to himself, seething with rage. 'By God, I'll make him pay.'

Alerted by the loud groans and curses; tasked by the first officer to oversee the work party on the floating dock, the Hawk's boson swung a thick knotted chord of rope into the palm of his broad calloused hand, as he snapped at the furious seaman,

131

'Get on with your work, you lazy dog! The Captain wants the repairs finished by sunset tomorrow, and yer mates will be needing that hot tar soon. Now before I lay into you, get on with it!'

Irish Jack seethed, but remained sullen and silent. Disobeying the boson, under the direct orders of the officer of the deck, would lead to a flogging. The scarred seaman's eyes narrowed coldly, but he kept his lips clamped firmly together, and remained silent. Defiantly, he bent down and picked up the steaming ladle. Limping painfully back to the cauldron, he began to sullenly stir the bubbling tar once again. No-one heard him swear an oath to himself; Quinn was going to pay for this. They'd see; he seethed silently, first chance he got...

Chapter Sixteen

Don Rodrigo fumed.

He listened with growing impatience and frustration to his assembled captains, as they reported their lack of results in the hunt for the English pirates. His warships had patrolled along the coastline, one hundred nautical miles; north and south of Boca Del Rio, but their search had proved fruitless. Companies of soldiers, who scoured the vast jungle, had returned exhausted, and empty-handed. It was as though his hated foe, Sir Richard Starkey, had made a pact with Satan himself, and simply vanished into thin air.

'Perhaps they have taken the Santa Juliana, and sailed for England, Excellence?' suggested one Captain.

'Yes,' said another, 'that would certainly explain their disappearance.'

Don Rodrigo shook his head doubtfully. His eyes narrowed with suspicion as he replied,

'No, I'm not so sure. Both ships were damaged, and they would have to put in somewhere to make repairs. With so many river deltas, coves and hidden inlets along the coastline, they could have made their ships seaworthy again in any one of them by now, and be lying in wait...'

Perplexed, the Captains looked at each other,

'Waiting? For what, Excellence?' enquired one of his officers.

Don Rodrigo let out a sigh. Was he really the only one who could see the danger? He was; he decided, surrounded by fools.

'Do you think it was pure coincidence that the English pirates arrived when they did? Gentlemen, Veracruz is a nest of spies in the pay of our enemies. They will know for sure that the treasure convoy is due to leave for Spain in a matter of weeks. Be of no doubt. Starkey and his wolves have come here on a mission to steal what rightfully belongs to our noble King. Trust me, gentlemen, their arrival now is no coincidence.

Realisation spread around the room.

'Of course, the treasure convoy!' murmured someone in Don Rodrigo's audience.

'Precisely that!' exclaimed the Governor, pounding his fist into his other hand. 'It is my belief that other English pirates will arrive very soon in the waters off the Yucatan Peninsula. They will probably rendezvous with Starkey's repaired ships far out to sea and ambush the convoy somewhere beyond the horizon,' Scowling, Don Rodrigo face was cold. 'And of course, gentlemen, it is our duty to stop them.' He began to pace back and forth. 'As your Governor, I have doubled the guard around the treasury.' He stared balefully at his officers. 'However, that is not enough. I want ships to patrol the horizon, right up until the moment the convoy is fully loaded, and ready to sail for Spain. At the first sign of an English flotilla, we will take every ship capable of carrying cannon, meet them in battle, and sink the pirate ships.'

The officers nodded their approval; these new measures were tactically sound, and glory awaited any involved in destroying such a threat to the Spanish enterprises in the New World.

'But what of the mule-train, Excellence?'

Don Rodrigo smiled thinly. 'Ah yes… the mule-train. It is time for you to know a great secret. Among the treasure it contains, which, of course, is considerable, is perhaps the greatest treasure of all. Our brothers in Peru captured a most remarkable Inca statue dedicated to their sun God, Inti. The idol is cast from solid gold, and I'm told its eyes are fashioned from huge rubies. It is so big, gentlemen, that it had to be split into pieces, and distributed among six mules to transport it.'

134

The Governor held up his hand, to quell the whistles and excited murmurings that erupted at his news. As their voices faded, he continued,

'Naturally, when this pagan idol arrives in Spain, it will be carefully reassembled, and then be presented to his Majesty in Madrid, as a personal gift from me, as Governor of his most loyal New World colonies.

Don Rodrigo paused, and inwardly smiled to himself. What needed he of letters of commendation from that old fool, La Valette, on Malta? To the Governor's certain knowledge, the Inca Sun statue was the greatest treasure ever recovered from the savages, anywhere in the New World. It's safe delivery would ensure him patronage and high favour from the King; having taken the credit for its capture and safe transportation. A gift of such magnitude would cement a powerful position in Phillip's Court, which lately, had become notorious for its intrigue, plots and bitter feuding between the families of various high ranking noble courtiers. When Don Rodrigo returned in triumph, a few years hence from the New World, he divined that Royal gratitude for such a sumptuous gift would protect him from the scheming machinations of his noble peers.

'Of course, I seek no personal reward for this,' he lied. 'But I pray to God that it will add to the King's majesty and prestige,' he added unctuously. 'The golden idol of Inti, the very essence of the Inca Sun God will be a vivid symbol of our victory in the New World; it will inspire awe and envy between all foreign ambassadors and dignitaries who attend our beloved King...' He crossed himself and clasped his hands together in feigned supplication. 'Even his Holiness, the Vicar of Christ in Rome will hear of its magnificence.' Burdened with such great responsibility, for the benefit of those who attended him, he let a sigh escape.

* * *

It was another boring day, patrolling along his lonely beat under the burning sun. The sentry, standing behind the crenelated stone battlements of Boca Del Rio's harbour fort, lifted his hand to shield his eyes from the dazzling glare, which reflected from the sparkling waters of the bay. He rested his pike on the gap between the stone battlements, and removed his heavy iron helmet. Wiping a hand across his brow, his eyes narrowed as he idly stared at the small boat several hundred yards away, which had been lazily fishing for the last hour in the mouth of the harbour. One of the local fishermen was standing in the boat, preparing to make another cast. The sentry watched as the net spun from the fisherman's hands, and landed with a muffled splash in the water beside the boat. As the mesh sank from view, the others in the boat remained where they were, and made no effort to help. *Lazy bastards*, he thought to himself. His attention was distracted suddenly, by rapidly approaching footsteps on the flagstones behind him. He turned and saw the officer of the guard, and his sergeant striding towards him.

It was agreed among the soldiers who guarded the fort, that their new officer was little more than a boy. It was their bad luck to be commanded by a well-connected stripling, fresh from Spain, who knew nothing, but was determined to carve out a name for himself. Hurrying to replace his helmet and recover his pike, the sentry didn't see the stinging blow coming, which suddenly cuffed him hard across his cheek.

'You know standing orders forbid the locals to fish here, don't you?' demanded the young officer impatiently. His face still smarting from the slap, the sentry snapped to attention,

'Yes Sir…but I thought…'

'*SILENCE!*' roared his young Captain. Turning to the sergeant he said angrily, 'Put this man on a charge for dereliction, then fire a warning shot at that damned fishing boat. Time we taught these savages a lesson in obedience.' A cruel

136

smile played across his face, as something occurred to him. 'There's a silver ducat for you, sergeant, if you can make them a real example, and sink their miserable little boat from under them.'

With a grin, the sergeant saluted and turned. As he hurried away to rouse a gun crew and carry out his orders, the officer turned his attention back to the unfortunate sentry.

'I will have discipline within my command. I'm going to make an example of you, you useless turd. I'll have the company mustered tomorrow morning, and see to it you are flogged...'

* * *

'There, Master! There's another one!'

As Fredrik hauled the empty net aboard, Quinn nodded excitedly towards the wooden barrel, bobbing at anchor in the waters of the port's narrow approach channel.

Richard saw it too. After an hour of secretly marking the depth of the seabed on Godshaw's chart, it was clear now why the Spanish had laid out the line of floating marker buoys. They marked a safe, straight route through the only deep-water channel, which avoided the treacherously shallow reefs on either side. The submerged outcrops seemed to grow from the sandy seabed almost everywhere in the sheltered waters between the harbour and the little offshore island.

Richard ground his teeth in frustration, 'Mark it on your chart Master Godshaw. We might as well...'

There was a sudden puff of white smoke from the stone fortress, and an echoing boom close behind it. With a mighty whoosh, a cannonball splashed into the water, less than twenty feet from the fishing canoe. The towering column of water cascaded over the boat, drenching its occupants. Hendrik nearly toppled overboard as Richard reacted instantly, and heaved the tiller hard over.

137

'They're onto us, Captain. They're trying to kill us!' screeched a terrified Godshaw, as he threw his hands over his head and ducked down as low as he could within the narrow confines of the dugout.

As the small boat turned, Richard smiled,

'No Master Godshaw, I don't think so. The Spanish have just sent us a warning...' He looked from one startled face to the next, 'it doesn't matter anyway. We're getting too close to their ships, and have outstayed our welcome. I think we have enough information...it's time to go!'

Chapter Seventeen

Richard planned to attack the mule-train after destroying the anchored ships in Boca Del Rio. It must be so, he thought, as it was clear to him that Don Rodrigo would certainly field every man he could, leaving no stone unturned to search out and recover the fortune, once Richard's crew had captured it. The repairs were on schedule; to his relief, the two ships were close to becoming seaworthy again, but knowing nothing of the jungle's interior; he needed Hendrik's help in formulating the ambush he planned shortly.

As his men began their last day of hammering and sawing, Richard called a conference among his officers on the quarterdeck of the Hawk. The jungle around the cove had come alive with the sun's first rays. The screech of hidden birdlife and the cries of distant monkeys filled the air as the officers assembled.

Stretched out before him was the hand-draw map of Boca Del Rio, which Hendrik and Godshaw had finished preparing after arriving safely back at the cove. Richard checked all were present, and then cleared his throat. He called the briefing to order.

'Gentlemen! ...Our repairs are almost finished. Tonight, we will attack the port of Boca Del Rio.' He lent across the chart and then looked up sharply. 'It will be difficult, but this is what we are going to do...'

Dark clouds scudded across a star speckled sky as the two ships cleared the heat and breathless humidity of the jungle. The crew, reinforced with volunteers from the escaped slaves, were spread thinly between the Hawk and the Juliana. They paused for a moment from their duties, and breathed a sigh of relief as the ships joined the slowly drifting current of the great river, which would take them within the hour to welcoming embrace of the open sea.

'Good to be away from that stinking rat-hole of a jungle, Master,' growled Quinn. He breathed deeply, savouring the cool river air as it filled his lungs.

Richard smiled. He too was enjoying the respite from the oppressive, claustrophobic atmosphere they had left behind them. Standing on the quarterdeck of the Santa Juliana, watching the sleek, unlit stern of the Hawk just fifty yards ahead, he called quietly over his shoulder.

'Steer a point to starboard, Quinn. We must keep close to the Juliana, or we'll lose her in the darkness.'

Quinn acknowledged the slight course change, and hauled on the great wheel to adjust their course. 'One point to starboard, Master.'

Richard lifted a hand in acknowledgement. He had ordered a total blackout of the exterior of both ships. Once they left the hidden cover of the cove, and entered the wide river delta ahead, they must not betray the slightest sign of their presence to patrolling Spanish ships. Being invisible, and using surprise, were the keys to success. Without them, Richard knew his crew, plan, and both his ships would be doomed.

Aboard the Sea Hawk, the crew were busy, clearing for action. Casks of black powder were carried up to the gun deck from the magazine, and the Hawk's guns were being loaded and prepared for the coming battle. Muskets were also unlocked from the armoury, and prepared by those skilled in their use.

Below decks, the Hawk's surgeon had lain out his medical instruments, and beneath the swinging light of the ship's lanterns, was busy checking the sharpness of his lopping knives and the bone saws he would need for the amputation of smashed limbs when the action started, and causalities began to arrive. His assistant sluiced down the small operating table with a

140

bucket of fresh seawater, and having mopped the floor, wandered off to the medical locker in search of fresh bandages.

* * *

In Veracruz that night, Don Rodrigo was holding a reception for the officers of the fleet, who would shortly depart for their distant homeland. He was determined that it would be a most opulent affair, designed to impress his honoured guests with its lavishness. In return, he would send stories of his success, wealth and prosperity to the Royal Court in Spain. The dining table groaned under the weight of the food his chefs had prepared. White coated servants stood ready to begin serving, when their master gave the signal. Others stood close by, carrying trays laden with goblets of fine wine for his guests. Beneath glittering chandeliers, soft music wafted in through opened glass doors; played by his accomplished troupe of musicians, who had setup their instruments on the cool stone veranda outside.

Dressed in his finest uniform, befitting the high office of Governor, Don Rodrigo formally welcomed each of his guests in turn, as they alighted from their carriages, and were announced. His guest list was not confined to nobles and the military, however. As was usual in such circumstances, naturally, he had also invited Bishop Acosta to enjoy the festivities. At the right moment, the Bishop would call down the Lord's blessings, to protect all those in peril, during the long, dangerous journey on which they would soon embark, in the service of their King.

Between his welcoming duties, Don Rodrigo scowled to himself. The Bishop would undoubtedly request more resources and money to complete the most opulent cathedral in the New World. His never-ending demands for labour and gold interrupted the Don's plans, but what could he do? Without the

141

Bishop's support, life could become very difficult in this God-forsaken wilderness.

Despite his vows of poverty, always eager to display the majesty of Holy Mother Church, Bishop Acosta arrived in a coach drawn by six beautifully groomed white horses. Their polished traces and gold-leaf adornments glittered in the torchlight as the coachman slowed his charges outside the palace's grand entrance. Stepping down from the coach, the Bishop was resplendent in his own finery; a full-length purple cassock of pure silk, and wearing, on his chest, supported by a thick chain fashioned from local gold, a jewel encrusted Cross. The Bishop stopped, and bowed towards his host with an ingratiating smile. He had business to discuss, but his request for another donation to support the construction of the cathedral, could wait until later.

'Good evening, your Excellence.'

Don Rodrigo returned the bow. 'Your Grace, it is always a pleasure...welcome to my humble house.'

* * *

Shrouded in darkness, the Hawk and Santa Juliana lay at anchor on a calm sea, less than a mile along the shoreline, from the entrance to the port of Boca Del Rio.

As the last of the skeleton crew from the Juliana scrambled aboard the Hawk, Richard called softly down to Quinn, who sat waiting patiently in the fishing canoe they had used to reconnoitre the harbour. Beside Quinn's tiny vessel, another canoe bobbed beside him.

'Is everything ready, Quinn?'

Quinn looked up at the dark shadow leaning over the guard rail, and replied,

142

'Aye master....' Quinn lent forward, and checked the bundle wrapped in oilskins at his feet, 'we're all ready down here.'

Richard glanced towards the lights of the harbour. If his plan was to work, Quinn's timing was everything. He would rather have been in the canoe with his servant, but responsibility weighed on his shoulders. If his plan was to succeed, he must remain aboard the Juliana. Returning his attention back to the canoes below, Richard hissed,

'Very well then, remember Quinn, watch for the lantern's flash in one hour...I'm counting on you, you rascal.'

Quinn nodded, although the gesture was lost to the darkness,

'I'll be ready, master.' He turned to the crewman in the other canoe and growled, 'cast off Silus, raise your sail and follow me as the wind takes you.'

As the two small boats disappeared silently towards the harbour, Richard walked across the quarterdeck to the other guardrail and cupped his hand to his mouth,

'Quinn's away, Will. We'll wait half an hour. Be ready to raise your anchor and follow me, when I give the signal.'

Aboard the Hawk, William raised his hand to his mouth and replied, 'we're ready and at your command, Captain.'

Richard turned away from the comforting silhouette of the Hawk, and picked up the heavy axe at his feet. Hefting it over his shoulder, he walked around the lengths of rope climbing up into the rigging above, and opened the companionway door. A faint spill of light shone out from the two lanterns which glittered just inside the door. Nodding with satisfaction, Richard closed the door, returning to the deserted quarterdeck, cloaked in its blanket of silence and darkness.

* * *

The glittering reception was going well. The noise of conversation and the laughter among his guests' had risen steadily, as goblets of wine emptied, and were quickly refilled by the attendant servants. Welcome compliments were gratefully received, as Don Rodrigo circulated between the nobles who were making the most of his generous hospitality. The Governor had been careful not to be cornered by Acosta, but to avoid him further, would, he feared, be taken as an insult by the Bishop. It was time to eat, so Don Rodrigo strode across the reception hall, and caught the eye of the head of the Inquisition in Veracruz.

'May I ask you to say Grace, Bishop?'

Acosta's eyes glittered. Handing his goblet to a passing servant, Bishop Acosta clapped his hands. As a respectful hush settled on the flushed faces of the Don's guests, the Bishop raised his hands in supplication before making the sign of the Cross. Clearing his throat softly, he called on high,

Father, Lord of creation and all things, we humbly beg you to bless this banquet…'

* * *

The gravel hissed and parted as the bow of Quinn's canoe grated on the shoreline. He quickly dropped the sail as the next small wave washed the little boat several feet further onto the sandy spit of land, on the far side of the harbour's mouth. Quinn leapt from the canoe, and grasping the bow, dragged it clear of the gentle breakers. Satisfied it was in no danger of being swept away, Quinn crouched down and listened intently for signs of discovery at his landing. He waited several minutes, but heard nothing. Relieved, he returned to the canoe, and recovered the oilskin bundle. Lifting it clear, he laid it on the sand and untied the twine which secured it. Removing the two torches it contained, he rammed their wooden shafts into the sand at his feet. His nose wrinkled as it caught the pungent odour of the tar

144

and oil which covered the wrapped hemp material of the torch's bulbous tip. Quinn snatched at the leather pouch tied around his neck, snapping the thin cord which held it there. Sweeping his head back and forth, to check again for signs of Spanish sentries, he opened the pouch and shook its contents into the palm of his huge hand.

On the other side of the dark harbour entrance, his shipmate, Silus, was doing the same.

Aboard the Hawk, Will Howard ordered his men to shorten sail. As the frigate began to slow, the Santa Juliana continued forward, its tall silhouette quickly swallowed by the darkness. The crew of the Hawk crouched at their guns, ready to pour supporting fire on the Spaniards, when they realised that they were under attack.

Richard stood at the Juliana's wheel. He had long since discarded the axe. It had served its purpose more than thirty minutes earlier, when he had used it to sever the Juliana's anchor rope. Parting the thick hemp with a dozen heavy blows, Richard had raced back to the quarterdeck, and arranged himself before the straining ropes which his crewmen had tied off after they had dropped anchor, a mile short of the harbour. Lifting the axe above his head, Richard swung it down onto the first cluster of ropes, which rose above him into the rigging. The axe severed several of them with the first blow. Heaving the embedded axe head free of the wooden deck, Richard swung again. The severed ropes twanged as they snaked upwards and disappeared. Seconds later, he was rewarded with the familiar flapping sound from above; it was the unmistakable sound of unfurling canvas.

Sweat ran freely from his brow, as he chopped steadily through the last of the retaining ropes. Casting the axe aside, Richard grasped the Juliana's great wheel, as the ship's sails filled with wind, and it began to nose its way slowly forward, towards the sleeping port of Boca Del Rio.

145

Quinn lay flat on the sand. He was watching for the Santa Juliana. The darkness would hide her, but with luck, if he kept really low, he would spy the dark outline of her bulk against the star studied horizon. It was a gamble, he knew, but his master's plan called for total surprise. If Sir Richard showed even the slightest speck of light before he was in position, the Spanish sentries patrolling the fort might see it and be alerted; they would immediately open fire on the wallowing galleon. Quinn shuddered at the thought. No, he counselled himself; he must stay low, and keep watching.

Richard peered into the darkness. To starboard, outlined against the pinpricks of light in the night sky, he could see a black smudge. It was the top of the palm trees growing on the tiny island, and the faint phosphorescence of the crashing waves of its shoreline. He could see nothing of the shore battery, or the men who manned it. There was no noise he could detect with straining ears, save the wind in the billowing sails, and the gentle creaking of the ship, as it sailed lazily towards the gap between island and harbour mouth. As he steered the galleon, something occurred to Richard. If he could see the island, anyone awake, guarding the battery, might be able to see the outline of his ship. Richard winced at the thought, but he knew there was nothing he could do about it. The ship was a Spaniard, with the bulk and traditional shape of a Spanish galleon. Perhaps, he hoped, if he was seen, it might confuse his enemies just long enough to get past them. The Latin phrase *'Iacta alea est,'* rampaged into his thoughts… Perhaps England's fate rested on these next moments. With a sigh, he knew the truth of it - Iacta alea est,' said it all - *'The die is cast!'*

Chapter Eighteen

Senses alert, Quinn's muscular body stiffened suddenly. He heard something. Not the scurrying of an animal, it sounded suspiciously like the scuff of a shoe, somewhere close by on the sandy spur where he laid quietly waiting.

The sentry sighed and grumbled to himself for the hundredth time since the incident with the fishing vessel. It wasn't his fault that the damned boat had sailed too close to the forbidden zone inside the harbour. Why all the fuss, he wondered? Now, just after dawn there was a sentence hanging over him of a rotten flogging. He kicked at another stone on the sandy beach. With a sigh, he tramped on as he neared the end of his lonely patrol route. To add insult to injury, he had been ordered to take Manuel's night duty as extra punishment, by that snot-nosed little shit of a captain. Life, he decided, was as cruel, as it was unfair.

Lying behind the canoe, Quinn's hand moved silently to the dagger on his belt. Breathing softly, he could hear the footfalls clearly now. Whoever it was, they were almost on top of him and must surely see the outline of his boat at any second.

The sentry stopped a few feet from where Quinn laid hidden. Puzzled at the sudden appearance of the canoe, he levelled his pike, and sought out its occupants. Satisfied there was no-one abroad, he raised the sharp point of his pike. The small boat offered no threat, the sentry thought comfortably to himself. He shrugged his shoulders in the darkness. It must have broken its moorings and drifted away from one of the fishing villages further along the coast, and washed ashore here, on this secluded stretch of beach. Pleased with his explanation, his mind turned to money. It should be worth a good few ducats, he thought, and as he'd found it, by right, it was his to sell. Grinning as he shouldered the pike, his spirits began to lift as he casually ambled up to the small vessel, to see if it contained anything of value.

With a muffled grunt, as the sentry bent forward, Quinn exploded from the ground behind the canoe; his dagger flashed momentarily in the starlight. The sentry's face filled with confusion and shock. He coughed as he dropped his pike. His throat filled with something warm as his hands flew to the gaping wound in his neck. Trembling fingers felt blood spray across them. Darkness closed around him and became absolute, as his fell forward while his life quickly ebbed away. The sentry was proved right; the world was cruel, and not a fair place at all.

Heart racing, Quinn stared down at the lifeless body at his feet. With a look of grim satisfaction, he sniffed as he wiped his blade on the dead soldier's tunic. Quinn took a deep breath and re-sheathed it. He looked away and peered into the darkness, in case the sentry was not patrolling alone. When he heard nothing, Quinn thoughts returned to his Master. Ignoring the body, he lay down again and wiped flecks of dark blood from his hands in the sand, and patiently continued his silent vigil.

Richard strained his eyes, trying to pierce the night's gloom. As best he could judge, he had sailed to a position equally between the island and the harbour mouth. It was where he wanted to be, but without solid reference points to take a bearing, the chart Humble Godshaw had drawn was useless to him, as he hoped for the best as he blindly navigated the Santa Juliana through the invisible shoals and reefs. Dead reckoning only worked to a point, even in broad daylight; at night he was playing a deadly game of chance, and he knew it. The Hawk sat higher in the water, but the lumbering Spanish galleon drew a deep draft. There was a very real danger that the Santa Juliana's keel would be torn out, if he allowed himself to stray from his present position. Without lights on the buoys marking the one safe channel, Richard offered up a silent prayer that his plan

148

would work. He ran to the companionway and wrenched open the door. Leaning inside, he snatched up one of the smoking lanterns, and hurried back to the wheel. Checking that his temporary absence had not caused the ship to drift, he held up the lantern, and shone its feeble light towards the landlocked port. After a heartbeat, Richard slowly lowered the lamp to the deck, hiding it from the land. He repeated the same procedure four times more, and then put his trust in luck, and the big Cornishman who he hoped was in position, watching and waiting for his signal.

He hadn't seen hide nor hair of the Spaniard's silhouette, lost as it was in the dark shadows which cluttered the island, but Quinn's sharp eyes saw the tiny spark of light out in the black waters beyond the harbour. He stared unblinking into the darkness as the light flashed on, then off, then on again. It was the signal he was waiting for. Quinn jumped up, and tore the flint and steel from the leather pouch. Turning to the embedded torches, Quinn struck the rough steel across the chunk of flint. He was rewarded with a shower of bright red sparks, which landed directly on the head of the nearest torch..., but nothing happened. With a curse, Quinn tried again, this time with more success. A blue flame spread quickly across the black sticky mess which coated the head of the upended torch. The flame quickly changed colour as the tar ignited. In moments, it spluttered and burned with a bright yellow flame, which spread to the other torch beside it.

With a muffled whoop of triumph, Quinn glanced towards the other side of the harbour entrance. His crewmate Silus had seen Quinn's torch begin to burn brightly, and had played his part perfectly, as he lit the two torches he had also brought with him in his own canoe.

149

To his delight, Richard saw the sparkling beacon of yellow light suddenly appear against the black backdrop. It was quickly followed by another, some hundreds of yards away to his left. Richard spun the great wheel urgently, and slowly, inexorably, the wallowing galleon responded to the abrupt change in course. It obediently headed towards the port, and the silent ships which lay at anchor within it.

The wind was freshening as Richard lined himself between the two specs of light. If he held his course, he should navigate safely through the reefs. Nerves strained to breaking point, he jumped at the sound of a loud bump, which reverberated through the ship's hull, but he relaxed instantly at the noise of something dragging and bumping along the ship's waterline. Richard smiled as he calmed. He decided that the good Lord was smiling down on him; to his relief, he had hit one of the floating marker buoys.

Leaving the torches burning brightly, muscles straining, Quinn pushed his canoe back into the water, and scrambled clumsily aboard. He snatched up an oar, and began paddling furiously towards the burning beacon on the far side of the harbour mouth.

Mouth suddenly dry, Richard grasped the great wheel tightly. Every second he avoided discovery brought him closer to the ships he must destroy. As the galleon drew level between the flaring torches, he heaved with all his strength, and turned the wheel towards the silent huddle of anchored ships. As he strained to fully turn the wheel, he wondered how Quinn made it look so damned easy. He smiled to himself at the thought of the giant Cornishman holding the wheel as if it were nothing but a child's toy. Casting Quinn from his mind, Richard straightened the wheel again, now he was steering directly at the darkened centre of the anchored Spanish ships. Richard tied off the wheel to keep the Santa Juliana on course, and walked quickly to the barrel on one side of the quarterdeck. Heaving aside the round wooden lid, he crouched down beside it and rammed his shoulder into its rough planking and iron staves. Pushing hard, the barrel began to tilt until it reached its point of balance. Richard strained again, and gave an extra heave. The barrel crashed over onto the wooden deck. The liquid contents, a noxious mixture of pitch, turpentine and gunpowder, spread quickly as it flowed across the creaking wooden deck. Richard splashed through the mix and heaved a second incendiary barrel over. The pungent fluid reached a cluster of barrels tied to the forward guardrail. It flowed on and soaked the foredeck and piles of stacked brushwood which were heaped around it.

An alarm bell began to toll from the direction of the fort. Richard knew he had been spotted. He marvelled at his luck, getting so close before the alarm was raised. As he ran to the stern of the Santa Juliana, he stopped and glanced forward beyond the ships flaming bow. The galleon was getting close now, but the bell had alerted the sentries aboard the anchored ships. There were confused shouts and a spluttering rattle of musket fire, but it would take a great deal more than a few one-ounce musket balls to change the fate of the frantically reloading musketeers.

Richard knelt down and struck flint to steel. The torch he placed there earlier spluttered and flared into life. Snatching it up and swinging the flaming torch over his head, Richard hurled it with all his might into the centre of the quarterdeck. As the burning torch struck the wooden decking, the incendiary mix burst into flame which a whooshing roar. Bright flames cast dark, dancing shadows as they leapt forward, and quickly spilled into the foredeck and engulfed the lashed barrels and brushwood. Richard felt the blast of heat on his face. He grinned with satisfaction at the flaring conflagration before turning and breaking into a run. A musket ball whacked into the main mast beside him, but he didn't slow. Urged on by shouts of alarm

151

behind him, and the splutter of wild musketry, his run became a sprint as he reached the ship's stern. Without breaking stride, Richard dived headfirst towards the dark waters, some thirty feet below.

Aboard the anchored galleons, it was a scene of utter chaos. Sentries yelled frantic warnings to each other as they pointed or fired haphazardly at the terrifying spectre of the burning ghost ship, rapidly approached under full sail. Few men were aboard guarding the ships; the bulk of the crews were ashore, making the most of the smoke filled harbour inns, and the pox-ridden whores who frequented them. If they missed their chance now, it would be a lonely, frustrating time during their long journey home.

In the last moments before the collision, panic took hold of the frightened men still aboard. There were no orders; the fleet's commanders were absent. Their noble captains and officers were away enjoying the more gentile hospitality of the Governor's reception, at his opulent palace in nearby Veracruz.

Richard coughed up a mouthful of scummy seawater as he surfaced in the eddying wake of the Santa Juliana. Eyes stinging, he trod water and turned to orientate himself. The stern of the fiercely burning galleon was some thirty yards from him now, but he could still feel its intense heat. The flames aboard had grown, even the lower sails were alight, casting a cherry-red glow across the harbour and the wooden hulls of the anchored Spanish ships.

The warning yells of the sentries changed to screams of terror as the heavy Santa Juliana smashed into the nearest ships with an ear splitting crash. Men aboard the nearest galleons were thrown off their feet by the powerful impact. Crackling orange flames began to leap from the doomed Juliana. They licked hungrily up at the rigging and tall masts of the nearest Spanish ships, as terrified sailors leapt overboard to escape the wave of blistering heat.

152

A few miles away, Don Rodrigo's reception was coming to an end. It had achieved everything the Don had desired. His guests had dined magnificently, and to his horror, almost emptied his well-stocked wine cellar. Thankfully, it was almost time to call for their carriages and bid his drunken guests farewell. The Governor however, was trapped outside on the veranda, locked in fierce conversation with Bishop Acosta, who had stalked him, waiting his moment, throughout the glittering evening.

'But I cannot take slaves from the mines, to labour on your cathedral. I don't have the manpower. What you ask is simply impossible!'

The Bishop scowled under a black sky lit by a million stars,

'What price can you put on doing God's work, my son?' He asked slyly, 'it is my sacred duty to spread His word amongst the heathens of this Godless land.' The Bishop clasped his hand together, almost in prayer, 'you know the Holy Scriptures command us to build His house wherever there is need? Our sacred duty is to reflect his love and divine glory to the faithful, and those yet to embrace Holy Mother Church.'

Don Rodrigo sighed. He knew he had no chance of denying the Bishop's plea for more help for the Church, or his damned half-built cathedral. It was a key part of the Bishop's plan to increase his flock, and must be built; but in the Don's mind, he was locked in a negotiation not to save his soul, but to limit the damage the Catholic Church would inflict on his own purse.

Sensing the Governor's moral weakness, Bishop Acosta pressed home his attack. 'Purgatory and damnation await those who refuse our Holy duties, my son...'

Don Rodrigo was about to reply when he saw the Bishop's face change suddenly, from unctuous piety, to something more quizzical. The ageing cleric was staring over the Governors shoulder.

153

'What is that light, my son? Down there, in the harbour?'

Don Rodrigo spun round. Colour drained from his face; his jaw dropped at the distant scene unfolding before him. A great red glow was coming from Boca Del Rio. Suddenly, there was an intense flash of light somewhere in its centre. Seconds later, they heard a distant, echoing boom.

'Don Rodrigo blinked in disbelief and horror. Only two whispered words escaped his lips,

'My God!'

* * *

Richard struck out with powerful stokes, away from the burning ships. Anchored close together, there was every chance, given the prevailing wind, that the fire would eventually engulf all the Spanish ships, before fire-fighting parties could be organised. Richard had ridden his luck so far, but if his plan was to succeed spectacularly, he decided when he began planning the attack; he must redress the balance, and inject at least some certainty into it.

Buried in the centre of the heaped pile of brush and barrels tied down on the foredeck, a fat keg of gunpowder was seconds from detonating. The blistering heat had burnt away most of its outer skin of thick oak staves. Suddenly, in a deafening roar of smoke and flame, the black powder exploded, lifting the burning pitch-filled barrels high into the dark skies above. Arcing through the blackness like fiery comets, they hurtled downwards and exploded among the tightly packed galleons. Filled with the remainder of the incendiary mix, and anything else that would burn, the blazing barrels quickly spread fire from one tinder-dry ship to its neighbour. The offshore wind added to the conflagration, fanning the chaotic orange inferno of burning decks and masts. Nothing could stop the towering flames now, the treasure fleet was doomed.

Out in the bay, Richard heard the explosion. He stopped swimming and turned to watch the fireworks. A single musket ball smacked into the water's surface, thirty feet from him. He didn't notice it, as all around, burning debris was falling into the bay from the star-studded heavens above.

Sacrificing the Santa Juliana was a shame, there would be no prize money, but it was the only way to destroy the Spanish ships. Richard had considered a hit-and-run attack into the harbour using his two ships combined firepower, but with the threat posed by the fort's guns, and the hidden battery on the island, the danger was too great. The bold option offered little chance of success, and indeed, the distinct possibility of disaster.

There was no pleasure on his face as he continued to stare at the inferno, just a grim satisfaction that his duty to England was part done, and as a bonus, he had extracted a morsel of revenge from his nemesis, Don Rodrigo. It wasn't enough, not nearly enough to avenge his beloved Miriam, but it was, he decided, at least a beginning. As the ships crackled and burned, Richard's mind was pulled from sorrowful contemplation by a sudden distant cry.

'Master, where are you?'

The captain of the Hawk smiled with relief. The big Cornishman was out there, somewhere close by. Richard stared into the darkness, searching beyond the waters lit by the flames behind him. Seeing nothing, he cupped his dripping hand to his mouth and cried out,

'Here Quinn!...I'm over here!'

Chapter Nineteen

The dark circles beneath Colonel Alveraz's eyes clearly displayed his exhaustion. His face and uniform was streaked with soot and smuts, having directed the forlorn efforts of the fire-fighting crews all night. A pungent odour of wood smoke seeped into the chamber from his ruined dress uniform. On the orders of the Governor, he had galloped to the harbour and organised the carousing crews, who had drunkenly spilled from the taverns when the alarm had sounded. Now, just after dawn, despite his fatigue, he had returned to the Governor's palace to make his report. He shook his head,

'I am sorry, Excellence. We saved only one ship from complete destruction. It can be repaired, I've been told, but the other ships were utterly destroyed by the fire.'

Don Rodrigo stared at him in silence for a moment as he listened to the awful news. His Governorship was in danger, and was becoming a waking nightmare. Through clenched teeth, he hissed,

'How did the fire start, Colonel?'

Alveraz sighed. 'It was a fire-ship, your Excellence. Somehow, it got over the reef and used the cover of the night to slip past our defences… I have no proof yet, but I suspect it was the Santa Juliana, and was the work of that heretic English pirate, Starkey.'

It was too much for the Governor. Don Rodrigo lost his temper and exploded with fury. He slammed his fist onto the desktop before him,'

'Curse that damned Englishman to hell!' Without a hint of his anger subsiding, he yelled at the exhausted Colonel, 'and what of our guards? Where were they?' Flecks of spittle flew from his lips. 'I want them arrested and put in chains, *NOW!*' he roared. His eyes narrowed. 'I'll teach them the penalty for sleeping on duty.'

156

'And their officers, Excellence?' Alveraz asked reluctantly.

'*Yes*, damn you! All of them, especially their officers!'

Despite his anger, Don Rodrigo's cunning mind raced. He needed scapegoats, and the men responsible for guarding the harbour would do for a start. He had not fully digested the enormity and ramifications of the previous night's attack, but when blame was levelled by the official enquiry, which, when the news reached Spain, was sure to be implemented by the Crown, he would do his utmost to ensure he was fully exonerated, and his family honour remained untarnished.

Beside him stood Bishop Acosta, who had listened to the Governor's angry rant in silence. Sensing the source of the Governor's distress, and with the issues of further funds and labour for the cathedral's construction rudely interrupted and as yet unresolved, he stepped forward and broke the uneasy silence which followed the Governor's outburst,

'Perhaps, Excellence, we have a traitor in our midst...? After all,' he mused thoughtfully, 'these diabolical English pirates navigated the dangerous reefs and found their way safely into the harbour;' he spread his hands, 'without mishap, or a single shot being fired. They must have gathered considerable intelligence beforehand, or else they would have been thwarted by nature and your excellent defences.' Calmly he added, 'Perhaps I could offer the services of the Church? Our Inquisition could expertly, ah, question the men involved, who may, after all, have conspired with the heretics?' He smiled helpfully and raised the palms of his hands slightly before him, 'But only, of course, if you think it a matter worth pursuing?'

Desperate for a way out of the maze of dishonour and ruin which might befall him, Don Rodrigo nodded enthusiastically,

'Yes, you are right, your Grace. Starkey must have had help...' He formally drew himself up and said, 'I charge you, Bishop Acosta, with the task of investigating this attack, and hunting down the traitor in our midst, if indeed, there is one.'

Bishop Acosta bowed his acknowledgement, and hurried away to organise the arrest of every man who was on official duties in Boca Del Rio, during the previous night. He smiled, cassocks flowing, as he swept from the Governor's office. His skilled torturers could arrange any number of confessions, once, of course; Don Rodrigo had quietly made the necessary manpower and donations to his building project.

Still standing in front of the Governor, Colonel Alveraz cleared his throat. He noted the order for arrests had lifted from his involvement, but he had not yet finished making his report.

Don Rodrigo looked up sharply at the tall Colonel. His voice betrayed his irritation,

'Yes Alveraz, what is it now?'

'I have a provisional casualty count, Excellence. We lost men last night.'

Don Rodrigo snorted,

'Well?'

'Eight are confirmed dead, Excellence, and twenty-three are missing among the crew members who were still aboard the fleet,' the Colonel's shoulders slumped with fatigue as he added, 'but we were extremely lucky. If the other sailors had not been ashore, and had been sleeping aboard their ships last night...'

Unconcerned with the fate of the dead and missing seamen, Don Rodrigo showed his disdain at the casualty figures with a wave of his hand.

'No matter... Was there any sign of Starkey, or his own ship?'

Alveraz looked troubled by the question.

Don Rodrigo's eyes darkened,

Well?

'A man was seen diving from the fire-ship's stern moments before it hit our ships. A sentry fired on the man when he surfaced, but couldn't see the man's face in the darkness.'

Don Rodrigo's nostrils flared as colour drained from his tightly clamped lips. Fighting to hold his growing anger in check, he announced,

'It was Starkey, Alveraz; I'm sure of it. I saw the man fighting in Malta. It would be a typical act of such a glory hunting swine.'

Alveraz nodded, but kept his opinion to himself. As a professional soldier, if it was indeed Starkey aboard the Santa Juliana, to his mind, it was an act of incredible bravery by a redoubtable enemy. Starkey was an adversary to be respected, not debased by callous insult.

Unaware of the Colonel's thoughts, Don Rodrigo demanded,

'What of his ship, man? Was that seen last night?'

Unsure of the truth, Alveraz nodded half-heartedly. 'A ship *was* seen soon after the time of the attack, Excellence, but on the far side of the island. I spoke to Admiral Ramos down at the harbour earlier this morning. He reported that his patrolling ships are not due back until later today or tomorrow. Not aware of this, in the darkness, the sentry assumed it to be one our own, returning from a patrol. He said it left shortly afterwards, and disappeared.'

The Governor slumped back into his chair. A nervous tick twitched around one of his eyes, as Don Rodrigo was consumed with bitter frustration, which was tinged with growing desperation. Without ships, he could not return the gold and silver to Spain in sufficient quantities. Interest on the loan he had negotiated with the Jews accrued daily. Non-payment was unthinkable; he must avoid foreclosure and retain his land in Spain, but he knew that he would be unable to service his debt as arranged. Profits would have to go, eventually, to cover the punitive charges and extra interest he would incur by defaulting on his next scheduled repayment. Becoming more desperate by the minute, the Don considered his only alternative. He could

159

use the small flotilla of warships, which guarded the coastline. Mercifully, they had been away on patrol when Starkey attacked, but they were small, and overloading them invited disaster. Many a treasure ship had been lost to storms and capricious seas, made too low in the waterline when overloaded with gold by greedy captains. If he did commit his remaining ships to return to Spain, he would need them all as it would take their entire load carrying capacity to get even close to the tonnage required, but that would leave him defenceless and vulnerable to attack from the sea. The English were becoming ever bolder, and a coordinated raid by English pirates in the coming days or months might mean losing everything stored in his treasury. Don Rodrigo cursed silently to himself. If there was a solution to his predicament, it stubbornly remained hidden from him. Just one man was to blame for his situation. Grinding his teeth, momentarily imagining the terrible, painful revenge he would extract from Starkey in the dungeons below his palace. He snarled as his eyes burnt like coals,

'By all the Holy Saints I want Starkey found, Alveraz, and by God, I want him taken alive…'

* * *

The Hawk had returned to the hidden cove.

Quinn and Silus had found their Captain. Having plucked him from the water, and after more than an hour of hard paddling, to their considerable and mutual relief, they had reached the preordained rendezvoused with the Hawk on the far side of Isla de Sacrificios. Richard had already discounted several alternatives; to his officers and crewmen's' dismay, he had decided to return to their humid, mosquito infested hiding place, where they had originally made repairs before launching the attack. When Humble Godshaw spoke up and raised his concerns, Richard reminded him, and his officers, that time was

160

against them. To find a better base from which to launch the raid on the mule-train might take days, which they did not have to spare.

As dawns first rays pierced the horizon, having posted extra sharp-eyed lookouts in the Hawk's crow's nest, Richard was satisfied that they had not been seen, as the Hawk slid slowly back into the wide river delta, before the green wall of the jungle gradually enveloped the Hawk, and hid her from view.

As the frigate dropped anchor in the hidden cove, below decks, Irish Jack was brooding. He was standing alone in the gloomy companionway, on guard outside the locked hold which held the Juliana's cache of silver bullion. He licked his lips as he thought of the pile of treasure, hidden just feet behind the bulkhead wall. By the flickering light of the lone candle beside him, he stared at the big iron padlock for the hundredth time since his duty began. He cared nothing for its ultimate destination, or the noble cause to which it would be put. If only, he thought, there was a way to break in, steal it and get away…Nothing occurred to Irish Jack, but perhaps, he thought slyly, there was another way?

Jack's plans of plunder were abruptly interrupted when one of the crew climbed down the narrow stairs.'

'Times up, Jack, I'm relieving you. Quinn said you are to muster with the water party up on deck.'

Irish Jack fumed, 'But I've spent the whole night here,' he jerked his thumb over his shoulder, 'guarding this lot.'

His crewmate shrugged apologetically, 'I'm just telling you what Quinn said, Jack. The master has ordered some the barrels we used to make the dock with, to be filled with extra freshwater for the voyage home.'

Irish Jack's shoulders slumped with resignation. Once again, Quinn had given him extra work. As he turned and began to climb the stairs, his crewmate failed to see the sly grin which

161

spread across his scarred face. Now was his chance, he thought, as one hand strayed innocently towards the handle of his dagger. He'd do for Quinn today, first chance he got, once they were alone together in the jungle.

The jungle had lost nothing of its oppressive heat or humidity, as the small party rolled the empty casks towards the nearest stream. Quinn's orders had been simple. He was to fill the barrels with clean, fresh water, and then return with all haste, before the Captain led almost the entire crew, supplemented by Hendrik's extra men, to take up their ambush positions, and wait for the arrival of the mule-train.

Serenaded from above by the usual choir of birdsong, the crewmen grumbled to each other, as they rolled the empty barrels along the track towards the stream. Quinn ignored their complaints and their curses. They were all dog tired after their nights work, and he knew they would have little time to rest before they reached the ambush point. Let them complain to thin air, he thought, it couldn't do no harm,

'Come on lads, not much further,' he growled, 'we'll be back aboard the Hawk before you know it.'

Unimpressed with Quinn's hearty encouragement, his men pushed on; they reached the stream minutes later. Stretching away their fatigue, each barrel was upended. With their lids removed, the handful of sailors began to slowly fill each one in turn, with wooden buckets they had brought with them.

The last barrel was almost full, when Irish Jack suddenly hissed a warning,

'*Quinn!* There, I think I saw something.'

Quinn looked up from the open barrel before him, 'What did you see?'

Irish Jack feigned concern and pointed, 'Something was upstream, I'm not sure. I saw a shape moving. It was big, like a man, and then it was gone.'

162

Quinn clicked his tongue with irritation. He didn't trust the man, but could not ignore Irish Jack's warning. Mindful that they had to get back quickly, he said with a sigh, 'All right, we'd better take a look.' He turned towards the other four men, 'Silas, you're in charge, go with him. The rest of you finish the filling, while they take a look.' The others nodded and returned to their duties as Quinn turned back to Irish Jack.

'All right then. Go and make sure we ain't being watched, and then get straight back,' his eyes narrowed suspiciously, 'and this had better not be a damned wild goose chase…'

Chapter Twenty

Aboard the Hawk, Richard was studying at a recently drawn map; he was flanked by Hendrik and surrounded by his officers.

The map showed the terrain of the surrounding jungle and the ancient route the Mayan trail cut through it. A heavily inked x showed their current position, beside the river, close to the coastline. Richard traced the line of the Mayan trail with his finger. He looked up and said,

'You know this track, Hendrik. Is there anywhere suitable which occurs to you, which we can reach that lends itself to an ambush?'

Hendrik stroked his beard for a moment as he reflected on Richard's question, and then he said,

'The trail is very old, Sir Richard, but now, because of the Spanish occupation, it is no longer maintained.' He shook his head slowly, as, inch by inch; he considered each section in turn. Finally, his finger paused on one particular spot. He looked up and said,

'The approach eastwards to this place is guarded by very steep hills, and covered on both sides by dense and virtually impassable jungle. His finger tapped down at one point on the trail, 'Here, Sir Richard. Here the land flattens. It is where a great swamp begins. The Spaniards must cross it very slowly and carefully, because there is mud and quicksand, just feet away, on either side. Should a man or mule stray and be caught wandering just a few paces off the track, they will surely be sucked under and die,' he shrugged, 'Perhaps two miles further on, where the swamp ends, the ground rises and begins to dry out.' Satisfied with the soundness of his decision, Hendrik nodded to himself, and looked up again. 'If I were going to attack, it would be after they emerge from the swamp, and before they reach the bridge.'

164

Richard looked up sharply. 'A bridge?…What bridge?'

The look on Hendrik's face was apologetic. He tapped his forehead with the palm of his hand,

'I'm sorry, no sleep has made me stupid. There is a deep gorge about half a mile beyond the swamp. It can only be crossed by using a very old rope suspension bridge, which the Mayans built long ago. I have seen it only once, but it is a marvel; a tribute to the Mayan's engineering skills. The gorge it spans is wide and very deep. Without making use of the bridge, a traveller must detour, perhaps, fifteen or even twenty miles through dense virgin jungle, to reach the outskirts of Veracruz.

Richard looked down at the map, and demanded,

'Show me where the bridge is…exactly.'

As Hendrik muttered to Master Godshaw, the scribe inked in the gorge and the bridge's location. Richard rubbed his chin, deep in thought,

'If we destroy the bridge first,' he said, 'and then ambush the mule-train after they leave the swamp, they'll have nowhere to run,' Richard looked up from the map and smiled grimly. 'Gentlemen, we'll have them caught like rats in a trap.'

Irish Jack moved quickly, knee deep and splashing softly against the gentle current of the stream. He called over his shoulder,

'It was up here I definitely saw something, It might have been a Spaniard spying on us.'

Silas followed close behind. He scanned the surrounding jungle, but saw no-one. The sailors filling the casks were quickly out of sight, as the two men followed the meandering course of the stream. Irish Jack turned as he waded through the cool water,

'Just a little further, whatever it was must have left some sign on the ground.'

165

Silus grunted. As Irish Jack was wading in front of him, the ageing sailor couldn't tell if the mud beneath the surface had been disturbed by the phantom, or by the truculent sailor who led. He had been looking carefully, but had seen no footprint or disturbance of the muddy stream banks on either side of them. Suddenly, Jack raised his hand and froze in the middle of the narrow stream. He turned and beckoned Silas forward, then pointed off to his right. Silus waded as quietly as he could, until he stood beside Irish Jack. His eyes narrowed suspiciously as he peered into the jungle and whispered,

'Well, what was it, what did you see?'

Jack pointed again, and said softly 'In there, I definitely saw a man looking back at me. It was a Spanish soldier, I'm sure of it.'

Silus awkwardly waded to the edge of the stream's bank. As he dragged his feet through the soft clinging mud, he stepped over the vegetation which draped the stream's edge and pulled aside a bush to get a better look. Intent on his search, he didn't notice Irish Jack behind him, or see the sailor's hand move to his belt and silently slide his needle-tipped dagger from its sheath...

* * *

'What of our route from here, Hendrik, how long will it take us, do you think, to get there?'

Hendrik shrugged. 'We have hunted many times as far as the Inca trail, Sir Richard...Beyond it, is the land of the Olmec people.' Hendrik's face suddenly darkened. 'We stay away from their territory; they guard it jealously, you see? Since the Spanish came, and began taking jungle people as slaves, the Olmec trust no-one. They were a peaceful people once, but the Conquistadors put an end to all that. Now, they are simply filled with suspicion and hatred towards anyone who ventures into their territory. They are dangerous enemies and true masters of

166

living in the jungle. They hunt in total silence with blow-pipes. The darts they fire are tipped with a deadly poison, which paralyses and kills in seconds. Their war parties take the heads of their victims as trophies. Somehow, they shrink them to a quarter of their original size.' Hendrik shuddered. 'We have tried to be friendly, and made a peace of sorts with them when we first established our colony. Hendrik nodded sadly at the memory,

'We do not venture into their land. It was agreed as a condition when we made peace with the Olmec. They would leave us alone as long as we respected their boundaries. Sadly, one of our hunting parties got lost, and they paid for their mistake with their heads.'

There was silence between the two men for several moments, before Richard put aside the murderous Olmec people and their land. With difficulty, he also suppressed any thought of the ghastly fate which awaited any who crossed into Olmec territory. He said,

'Tell me more about the jungle between us and the trail.'

Hendrik smiled weakly, pleased to be distracted from the loss of his friends.

'There are some hills to cross, and the jungle is thick, but we know the easiest trails. I would think that if we travel light, we can be at the edge of the swamp in, maybe five hours?'

Richard nodded. The mule-train was due any day now, and the sooner they laid their ambush and attacked, the sooner they could complete his plan to thwart the Spaniards.

'How many mules, and how many soldiers are set to guard them,' he asked.

'Last time the mule-train arrived, there were about one hundred mules, and perhaps forty soldiers to protect them during the journey.'

Richard looked surprised.

'So few?'

167

Hendrik smiled. 'Between the mines of Peru and Veracruz, there are no brigands, only many, many miles of jungle wilderness, my friend. The soldiers are there to guard against occasional attacks by small bands of natives, whose territory they must cross.'

It was Richard's turn to smile. The element of surprise would be with them, and worth at least a hundred men.

'What of the muleteers? How many will there be?'

Hendrik shrugged again. 'Each one leads a string of perhaps five mules, so, perhaps around twenty in total?' Richard's eyes narrowed.

'Will they stand and fight?'

Hendrik shook his head. 'I doubt it. They are unarmed civilians who are hired to tend and lead their mules; they are certainly not soldiers. If their lives are in danger, I think they will run,' he added with a reassuring smirk.

Richard was pleased with what he had heard. Time was against them, but his men were tired, and tired men made mistakes. No, he thought, It would be nightfall in a few hours, not enough time to reach the trail. Richard made his decision. Even with Hendrik's help, he didn't want to risk blundering around in a pitch-black jungle, trying to find the track, or the great bridge, in the dark. A better plan was to let them all get a good night's sleep. 'We will begin our march at dawn, Hendrik. Please tell you men, there can be no going back after we strike. Once we are done with the mule-train, Hendrik, and safely returned to the Hawk, we load everything aboard and set sail for England immediately.'

Hendrik let out a sigh. He nodded his understanding and brightening, he said, 'And then at last, I to can go back, and begin the search for my beloved wife and children…'

Irish Jack grinned to himself, as he looked down at the lifeless body of his crew mate. It was too easy to stab his blade

168

between the man's shoulder blades. Old Silus made no sound as he fell, but shock and pain were clear to see on his frozen face. Jack sneered. He just wished it had been Quinn who had come with him. Lying face-down on the muddy bank, blood oozed from the deep wound in Silus' back. Irish Jack was startled suddenly by the cry of a bird, high above in the canopy. He glanced nervously back along the stream, but no-one was there. Satisfied he was in no immediate danger of discovery; he rinsed his bloody hand and knife in the stream, and wiped the glistening blade on Silus' rump to dry it. Casting a last glance back downstream towards the hidden work party, Irish Jack struck out into the jungle.

Using the dense vegetation as cover, it would be a simple matter, he thought, to creep around Quinn and the others. He'd soon angle back to the stream, and then follow it down to the sea. It would be a simple task to avoid getting lost, by following the route of the Santa Juliana's crew along the coast to Veracruz. If he travelled through the night, he'd be there around dawn tomorrow. Plenty of time, he thought with a sly grin. Irish Jack wanted a share of the silver aboard the Hawk, and reckoned he would be well rewarded by the Spanish when he led them to the hidden cove. It was disappointing, he thought, that he hadn't personally had the chance to finish Quinn, but it wasn't the end of the world. He'd happily settle for a front-row seat, when Spanish troopers returned their captives to Veracruz, and they put a noose around his neck and hanged the big Cornish bastard.

Keeping low, Irish Jack silently skirted the work party, re-joined the stream, and then he began to wade quietly through the shallow water towards the sea.

Further upstream, Quinn hammered the last wooden lid with his massive fist, locking it firmly onto the barrel before him. Satisfied that it was sealed properly and his task was complete; he looked up. He was growing more concerned by the minute; however, as Irish Jack and old Silus had not returned. He turned

169

toward his men, 'You start rolling the casks back to the Hawk, lads, while I go and see what's happened to Silus and Jack.'

Unaware that anything was amiss, the others nodded and turned to their task. Quinn watched them go, and then began to wade upstream. Moving quickly, he drew his scimitar.

It didn't take him long to find Silus' lifeless body. The wound in his back told Quinn everything he needed to know. Having quickly searched the immediate area around the body, he discovered no blood trail or signs of a struggle. There was only a single set of footprints leading from the body into the jungle, but no other trace of Irish Jack. Deeply disturbed, Quinn struggled with what to do next. Should he set off in pursuit of Silus' killer, or return to the Hawk and warn his master? Frowning and alone, Quinn agonised with the decision he must make, as he looked around him. No, he decided abruptly, he must raise the alarm and warn the others. If he did strike out into the jungle alone, and strayed from the killer's tail, he faced the prospect of getting lost, or even ambushed. His duty was to tell Sir Richard what had happened; his master would know what to do.

Quinn retraced his steps, and lifted Silus' limp body over his broad shoulder. He'd not leave a good shipmate remains out here in this Godless wilderness. If there were time, he'd see Silus to his eternal rest, and bury him as any Christian man should.

Chapter Twenty-One

Quinn laid old Silus' body gently down on the sandy beach of the cove. Shaking his head as he stared sadly at his murdered shipmate, Quinn brushed aside the sentry's anxious questions and strode up the gangplank onto what was left of the floating jetty. He saw Lieutenant Howard standing nearby with his back to him. Striding towards him, Quinn rumbled,

'Beggin pardon Mister Howard, sir, but I need to talk to Sir Richard, real urgent.'

Will Howard turned and stared at his Captain's servant. The expression on the giant's face screamed only one word... *Trouble!*

'What's the matter, Quinn?' as he spoke, Will Howard glanced past the giant at the prone figure and the sailors gathering around it on the beach behind him. Confused, he demanded, 'What in God's name has happened?'

'When I found old Silus, he was dead, master. Knifed in the back, he was, and Irish Jack nowhere to be seen.'

Standing in his cabin, Richard frowned. With a crewman murdered, and another missing, everything had suddenly changed for the worse. Richard knew Irish Jack's reputation aboard as a troublemaker, and of the bad blood which existed between him and Quinn. Suspecting treachery, Richard said,

'His tracks led off into the jungle, you say? Which way did they go?'

Quinn's face darkened, 'Hard to say, Master. The jungle was real thick where it happened, but if it was me, I'd have followed the stream towards the coast to avoid getting lost.' As an afterthought, he added, 'the going would have been much easier, and faster if he went that way.'

Richard nodded. What Quinn said made complete sense. There could only be one destination on Irish Jack's mind after he killed the old carpenter. He must have been planning his treachery for a while, and used this opportunity to escape. With nowhere else to go, surrounded by hundreds of miles of wilderness, Richard was sure that the renegade Irishman must have set off towards Boca Del Rio, to alert Don Rodrigo of their presence.

Richard turned to Hendrik, who had been speaking to him when Will Howard had ushered Quinn urgently into his cabin, moments earlier,

'Without signs of a struggle, and only one set of footprints leading away from old Silus' body, we must assume that Irish Jack is the culprit. It follows that he has turned traitor, and will try to earn gold, and freedom, by selling out and informing the Spanish of our current location,' with a sigh, he added, ' and tell them of my plan to attack the mule-train.'

Quinn stared down at his feet. He shook his head sadly and said,

'Curse me for a fool master, I'm so sorry, I should have seen this coming. That dark-hearted bastard tricked me into sending him and old Silus into the jungle. I should have gone with him, in Silus' stead.'

Richard looked at his servant and shook his head, 'No Quinn, don't punish yourself. You're quite wrong to take the blame; it's not your fault at all. None of us could have foreseen this coming. If you had gone into the jungle with Irish Jack, it would be your body lying on the beach.' He turned to Hendrik and Will Howard, 'The traitor has a good head start, and I see little advantage in searching the jungle for him,' Richard's expression was grave, 'We'll never find him now, but it will take a long time for him to reach Veracruz on foot. He'll not reach the Spanish before sometime tomorrow, so we are in no immediate danger of discovery. Clearly, it would be prudent to

172

move the Hawk today, and abandon this place forever. We'll have to take the Hawk back out to sea and try to find somewhere else to hide her, while we strike out and ambush the mule-train.' Determined not to be thwarted, Richard hardened his resolve as he looked directly at his first officer, 'I want you to go and search out Master Godshaw. Tell him to bring every chart in his possession to my cabin in half an hour. In the meantime, I'll make preparations to raise the anchor and leave.' He turned to Quinn. As his shipmate, I want you to take a couple of his friends, and see to it that old Silus' is properly buried.'

Quinn nodded eagerly,

'Yes, master.'

Letting another sigh escape him, Richard added, 'Hendrik, I need you to stay here, and help me find somewhere else to take the Hawk.'

'Here, Sir Richard. Here is an ideal spot to hide the Hawk.' Hendrik's finger stabbed down onto the chart laid out before him.

'Why do you advise this point?' Richard asked.

'It is a natural harbour, but well hidden from the sea. There is a waterfall on one side, and a natural path leading up to the jungle on the other. We call it the Bay of Gulls. My people know it well; we have hunted the cliffs which surround it many times for bird's eggs.'

Richard frowned. 'How far is it from the Inca trail?'

Hendrik grinned. 'That's the beauty of it, don't you see? The trail winds through the jungle, closer to the Bay of Gulls than where we are now. It is also further away from Veracruz.'

Richard nodded, as Hendrik continued,

'After we climb out of the bay using the track, it will take,' he pursed his lips and shrugged, 'no more than an hour to reach the trail.'

173

Richard was convinced. The Hollander's advice has been invaluable so far, and he saw no reason to question his judgement now. He said,

'Very well then, Hendrik, it sounds an ideal place.' He turned to his first officer. 'Make sure that Quinn and the burial party are back on board, Will. Then get the boat parties into the water and we'll tow the Hawk away from this cursed place for the very last time. When we reach the main river, we'll sail immediately for the Bay of Gulls.'

It was Will Howard's turn to frown.

'In broad daylight, Captain?'

Richard nodded. With a knowing sigh, he said. 'We have no choice, William. If we are to be in position to march on the track at first light tomorrow, we must anchor in safety before dark tonight.' He added, 'then we'll sleep.'

Will Howard nodded. He knew his captain was right, but there was always a danger from patrolling Spanish ships. Resignation spreading across his fatigued face, he said softly,

'God be with us then, Sir Richard.'

Richard nodded grimly, 'Aye Will, I pray He is…'

* * *

His spirits soaring as he put ever more distance behind him, Irish Jack grinned smugly to himself. The going was much easier than he had expected and he was making good time following the meandering route of the stream. He felt confident he would easily reach the coast well before last light. In the oppressive heat, he stopped for a moment, turned and stared back upstream. Senses straining, he saw naught to concern him, as he stood very still, listening intently for the slightest sound of pursuit. There was nothing, save the wind gently rustling the canopy high above and usual sounds of the insects and creatures that lived in the jungle. Grinning broadly, he lent forward and

174

with a satisfied sigh, scooped up a handful of crystal-clear water to refresh himself, before wiping his hand across his face, and resuming his journey towards the sea.

As he waded knee deep through the cool water, Irish Jack's mind wandered as he began imagining the delights his reward would bring. The Spanish, he decided, would harbour no malice towards him, he wasn't English after all. The opposite was true; he thought. He knew they'd be very grateful for the intelligence he would lay before them. He was happy to sell them the location of the Hawk, its crew, and their high and mighty English captain. Perhaps there would be extra gold, when he told of Starkey's plan to attack the mule-train? Why not, he asked himself self-righteously? He had no ties or friends aboard the Hawk. It was just another ship, in a long line of vessels where he had grabbed what he could to survive. Justification for turning traitor came easily. Born of lowly Irish Catholic stock, he felt no loyalty towards his protestant Queen, only deep-rooted hatred. The heretic bitch had persecuted his church, and sent English soldiers to crush rebellions over the water, on more than one occasion in his own lifetime. Many a poor Catholic peasant had died at their hands. Irish Jack bared his teeth in a snarl of memory, then hawked and spat into the undergrowth, loudly cursing memories of blood spilt in failed rebellion, but also vile oaths directed at the English Queen, whose bloody hands orchestrated so many deaths and executions of his own people and kin, in the hidden settlements and isolated farms of his mist shrouded, bog-ridden homeland.

* * *

As the drifting current of the great river gathered the Hawk into its welcome embrace, Richard ordered his boat's crews back aboard. Men stood ready, balanced in the tall yards, awaiting their captain's signal for the main sails to be unfurled.

175

In his palace in Veracruz, agreement between the two leaders had been reached on the cathedral's completion. Their business done, Don Rodrigo sat back comfortably and listened as Bishop Acosta began his account of the treasonable crimes his priests had uncovered.'

When he had finished explaining his report, Don Rodrigo nodded with satisfaction. The alleged culprits had died under torture at the hands of the Inquisitors, but in triumph, to seal their bargain the Bishop held in his hand, the guilty men's duly signed confessions.

'It was a great shame neither man survived their examination,' Bishop Acosta said sadly, 'but of course, as they admitted their guilt, your own men are completely exonerated.' The Bishop turned and stared out of the bay window. In the distance he could see the scaffolding which surrounded the half-finished cathedral. Smiling to himself, he continued,

'It is strangely fitting but somehow rather convenient that they are both dead; now of course, neither can recant their confessions.' He turned and held up the rolled parchments. 'They both admitted being in the pay of the English, and confirmed that they passed on information crucial to the attack on the harbour.' He stepped forward and handed over the scrolls to the Governor with a slight bow,

'I believe, your Excellence will wish to include these documents, when you make your written report to Madrid, on the pirate's attack,'

Don Rodrigo smiled as he gratefully accepted the two scrolls from the Bishop. He said nothing as he unrolled one slowly, and began to read the flowing script, written out by one of Acosta's priests. He glanced down at the prisoner's signature at the bottom of the document. It resembled the track left by a dying insect, which had crawled across the parchment. The Don's eyes flicked up from the confession as he nodded with satisfaction. A shackled man, excruciatingly tortured for hours

176

would admit to anything, he mused, if enough pain was administered, with rack, white-hot iron rod, and the myriad of other devices the Inquisitors used to extract the truth; whatever they decided it should be.

With these neat confessions, the Governor mused; culpability in anything associated with the destruction of the treasure fleet was no longer his concern. Two unfortunate and quite innocent Portuguese sailors, arrested by his soldiers in a waterside tavern, had become, with the assistance of the Inquisition, the scapegoats he desperately needed. Overall, his honour and position as Governor were now relatively safe, and as it transpired, well worth the inflated price from his own purse he had just agreed with the cleric standing before him.

With a sly and knowing smile, Don Rodrigo raised the confessions and nodded towards the Bishop,

'You are to be congratulated, your Grace. Your Inquisitors have done most excellent work.'

Bishop Acosta lifted his hands and eyes towards the chamber's ceiling. Equally pleased with the bargain he had negotiated, he lowered his eyes, genuflecting and clasping his hands together. Smiling, but with sad, troubled eyes, he sighed,

'Ah!...Such is the heavy burden I must bear to do God's sacred work here on earth, my son.' The Bishop made the sign of the cross towards Don Rodrigo, and whispered his final word on the matter, to seal their pact, forever,

'*Amen!*'

* * *

Lost to a private world of plotting and scheming, now only minutes from reaching the sandy coastline, Irish Jack's mind was intent on savouring the rich rewards which would soon be his.

He failed to notice something huge and terrible lying hidden amongst the submerged vegetation, which grew

177

luxuriantly at the side of the narrow stream. Skin beautifully patterned in camouflage hues of green and brown, it lay perfectly still just inches below the rippling water, lost from view in a gently wafting bed of weeds. Breaking the surface only occasionally to breathe, the ancient creature had lain hidden in ambush for days, waiting patiently for its normal prey of wild pig or deer to abandon natural caution and approach the stream to slake thirst in the cool, tempting waters which presently concealed it.

As he drew level, in a great maelstrom of spray, the water beside Irish Jack suddenly erupted and boiled as the huge anaconda reared up, exposing its open mouth, filled with rows of needle-sharp teeth. Jack had only a heartbeat to react; in the confused chaos of the snake's explosive strike. He was too slow to avoid its gaping jaws, which bit down and clamped tightly onto his shoulder. It happened so fast, there was no time to scream with the pain or terror which now engulfed him, as the massive serpent began to wrap its muscular coils around Jack's thrashing body. He tried desperately to reach for his knife, but his hands were immobile, trapped among almost thirty feet of slithering coils, whose girth was as thick as his own torso. Filled with panic and horror, Irish Jack struggled violently to break free, but the anaconda was too strong.

The massive weight of the snake's enveloping coils toppled Jack onto his side; he crashed down into the foaming water with a mighty splash, but his continued struggles failed to shed the snake's tightening coils.

Fighting to keep his dripping head above the shallow surface, gasping for air, Jack felt the hungry monster release its teeth and jaws from his shoulder. Blood flowed freely from the wounds, mixing with the mud and water which pooled and eddied around him. The massive snake's body shuddered as it increased the constriction on his helpless body.

178

Just inches from Irish Jack's contorted face, the great snake flicked out its forked tongue; tasting the air and watching its next meal with cold, unblinking eyes. Every time its victim breathed out, the snake reacted and the pressure of its powerful vice-like grip increased. All too quickly, each shallow gasp became an individual struggle of survival. Even Irish Jack's racing heart was struggling to pump life-giving blood around his slowly crushing body.

The unrelenting pressure around him was now so immense; his failing strength diminished as rapidly as the light began to fade in Irish Jacks bulging eyes. One by one, his ribs began to give up their struggle, splintering and cracking inside his chest with the reports of muffled pistol shots.

A last hurrah of anger surged through him as he tried to spit defiantly into the giant snake's coldly indifferent face, but instead, only choking, gurgled gasps escaped his purple lips.

Final thoughts floated dreamily through his oxygen starved brain; fragmented memories of his long-dead mother, and the gold and silver he would never see. Only he heard his mind cry out; a silent, visceral scream which echoed inside his head.

As the haunting sound slowly faded, he felt himself slipping into the cold void of oblivion. He knew in his last few moments, he had paid the ultimate price for his treachery.

The great serpent's scaly coils tightened once more, as they mercilessly crushed the last trace of life from Irish Jack's trapped and broken body.

Chapter Twenty-Two

'Drop anchor!'

Moments later, with a rumble and mighty splash, the great iron anchor broke the surface of the crystal-clear waters, and sank quickly to the sandy bottom of the hidden lagoon.

Surrounded by tall cliffs and the cries of nesting seabirds, the coming night had begun spreading its shadows across the Hawk, as its top-men finished furling the sails and securing them tightly to the horizontal yards attached to each tall mast.

Satisfied that all was in order, and the Hawk was safely anchored and secure, Richard turned to William Howard, who stood in attendance behind him,

'We should be safe here, Will, but just in case, I want lookouts posted straightaway, up on the cliffs at the mouth of the lagoon. They are to bring word to me instantly, at the first sign of Spanish ships.' Richard looked upwards and watched the swirling flight of a gannet, as it slowed and landed awkwardly on a rocky ledge, high above them. Turning back to his first officer, he said, 'See to it that everyone is well fed tonight. Apart from the watch, I want the crew fully rested. If we are to beat Irish Jack and the Spaniards to the mule-train tomorrow, I want just a skeleton crew left aboard, and everyone else assembled on the beach, fully armed and ready to move just before dawn. Is that clear?'

William Howard nodded. With a knowing look, he said, 'Yes, Sir Richard. I know what to do. I'll pass it on to Hendrik, and make sure everything is prepared as you require, and the raiding party is put ashore, armed and ready, just before first light…'

* * *

After his meeting with Bishop Acosta, as the night began to creep over his palace, Don Garcia sipped from a goblet of chilled wine as he sat alone in his office chamber. He was engrossed, mulling over plans for the hiring of merchant ships, to transport the fortune his treasury contained. It would take precious time to assemble a flotilla of the size he required, and would cost him dearly, but it was the only way to save himself, and his estate in southern Spain from foreclosure and ruin. A soft rap on the door disturbed his train of thought.

Fernandez entered holding a burning taper and bowed, 'May I begin lighting the candles, Excellence?'

The Governor nodded, and swept his hand absently towards some of the expensive beeswax candles which adorned ornate candelabra placed strategically around his office. Don Garcia watched in silence as Fernandez began his nightly duty of illuminating his master's office. Suddenly, a thought occurred to the Governor,

'Fernandez, when you have finished, send word to Colonel Alveraz. I will personally lead a detachment of cavalry tomorrow morning, find the mule-train, and escort it on its final leg, back to the safety of Veracruz.'

Pausing from his duties with the smoking taper, Fernandez turned and bowed slightly,

'Of course, Excellence, I shall see to it.'

Don Garcia smiled to himself as his servant finished lighting the candles and left to carry out his orders. Although there was no real danger, taking personal charge of the security surrounding the mule-train would look impressive, and sit well with Madrid, when his all-important report concerning the attack by English pirates arrived, carried by the repaired galleon he would shortly order to set sail for Spain, when it was fully repaired. Although the ship would be, perhaps, dangerously overloaded, he could afford to use it to save his skin. It would buy him breathing space. He could, at least, send several tons of

181

gold to pay the King his due, and keep the damned Jews off his back. He hoped that the addition of the incredibly valuable gift of the Inca Sun idol would help assuage any doubt as to his competence as a New World Governor, in the eyes of King Phillip. It was the one vital keystone in his plan of recovery. Although certainly now a bribe, he was sure the King would accept it. A gift of such magnitude should allow Don Garcia the time he needed to put the attack behind him, increase output from the mines and prosper, so far from Spain.

* * *

As the sun began to rise, Richard stepped down in the half-light, from the boat which had brought him ashore. William Howard and his crew, standing patiently on the sandy beach, fell silent as he climbed onto an outcrop of rock and addressed them,

'Well men,' he began soberly as he drew his sword,

'Men, you all know why we are here today. England desperately needs the money carried in the mule-train, to build ships and defend our shores against the vile Spaniards, who plan to use it to invade our homeland. They won't stop there though; oh no, they will lay waste and burn our settlements and hamlets, ravish our women and enslave our children...' Richard nodded theatrically; he must use every trick he knew to light the beacon of resistance and get their Anglo-Saxon hearts pounding. He continued, 'We have already singed King Phillip's beard with our attack on Boca Del Rio, but now, we need to finish the job.' Richard paused, and let his words sink in. Seeing heads beginning to nod and hearing affirmative mutterings among the crew, he held up his hand. His voice echoed across the cliffs which surrounded the lagoon, sending dozens of nesting seabirds' squawking noisily skywards,

182

'Now is our chance to delay Phillip's invasion, and hold him at bay until England is ready for him.' Richard's eyes blazed as he roared, 'so what do you say, my brave lads. Do we run away with the job half done, or do we defend our homes and families, and snatch the riches from those who would dare attack us?'

A savage grin broke across Richard's face as he raised his sword above his head. The blade glinted in the first rays of the sun,

'Now tell me lads...What say you? Will you defend Good Queen Bess, and our beloved England?'

To a man, the crew roared out their approval. Cheering wildly, forgetting past promises of rich reward, Quinn and his shipmates waved sword and musket aloft, bellowing bloodthirsty defiance at Catholic Phillip, his hated Inquisition and all those who would dare invade their precious island home.

Death to Phillip!

'Aye!' the crewmen wildly replied, *'And death to Spain!*...

* * *

Don Garcia began to regret his decision within a mile from the outskirts of Veracruz. Sweating freely under his armoured breastplate in the early morning sun, he held his bridle tightly, as he led his horse up the steep rocky path. Behind him, his cavalrymen were also on foot, each of them leading their horses up into the hills which separated them from the mule-train, which lay somewhere ahead. Don Garcia had chosen to ignore the advice of Colonel Alveraz to take a detachment of foot soldiers along the ancient path. The Governor knew better, but now he was paying the price.

His exit from the palace courtyard had been a grand affair. The city's entire garrison had been turned out to salute their brave Governor, with all the pomp and ceremony due to their

183

supreme commander. Alveraz had watched the mounted column depart, but reservation clouded his face as the last of the small cavalry detachment trotted its way through the crowded streets, and departed through the city gates.

Beside him, Admiral Ramos noted the Colonel's concerned expression,

'What is the matter, Miguel; why is there worry on your face?

The Colonel shook his head,

'I told that arrogant fool the track was not suitable for riding horses, but he wouldn't listen. The whole point behind the mule-train is the Mayan path through the hills and jungle was never made for carts or horses. It is littered with deep ravines, rockslides and steep climbs. I commanded the shipment from Peru last year, and it is no easy task, believe me. The only animals that can navigate the track are mules, and they struggle sometimes.' Exasperated, he added, 'that's why we use them exclusively as beasts of burden, for God's sake.'

Admiral Ramos shrugged, and patted the Colonel's forearm,

'Perhaps, on your own initiative, you should follow him with a detachment of soldiers?'

Alveraz stared over the city's rooftops, at the jungle shrouded hills beyond,'

'No. I have been ordered to stay here and take command of Veracruz, until Don Rodrigo returns.'

There was silence between the two commanders until Admiral Ramos spoke again,

'Well, at least Don Garcia has taken full command of the expedition.'

A quizzical look replaced the concern on Alveraz' face,

'So?' he enquired impatiently.

'So, if things go wrong,' Ramos grinned slyly, 'which they often do under Don Garcia's inept Governorship; we, my friend,

184

are safely under orders here in Veracruz, and will not be held to blame.'

Chapter Twenty-Three

Led by Hendrik, Richard, Quinn and the crew of the Hawk trudged in single file through the jungle as the day's heat increased. Battling the humidity, sweating and grumbling, his men slithered and fell in the sopping mud of the animal track, as they struggled to keep up. Several times during the journey, Hendrik had suggested they stop and rest, but Richard had urged them onward,

'We must hurry, Hendrik. If Irish Jack has raised the alarm, which he surely will have by now, we must hit the convoy and vanish before that swine, Garcia, sends reinforcements to escort it to safety.'

Hendrik could only nod. He saw the hatred burning in the young Englishman's eyes whenever he spoke the name of his nemesis. One thing was certain in the Hollander's mind. He had no intention of getting in the way of the bitter blood feud which existed between Sir Richard and the Spaniard.

When Hendrik signalled another halt at the junction of two tracks, Richard stared hard at the Hollander. Before he could speak, Hendrik held up his hand and said quickly,

'This is where we must split up, Sir Richard. If you still wish to cut the rope bridge, you must take the right fork, while the ambush party takes the left.

Richard nodded,

'Yes, it must be done. When we attack the mule-train, I don't want to be counterattacked by soldiers coming from Veracruz, or be pursued through the jungle while we take the treasure back to the Hawk.'

Hendrik said,

'Very well, Sir Richard. I have hunted this area several times, so I will guide you to the rope bridge myself. My men can lead your crew to the Mayan track.'

Richard signalled to William Howard, who hurried up to the head of the column,

'Will, Hendrik's men will guide you. Take the crew to the Mayan track, and set up the ambush as we discussed. We'll join you as soon as we are done with the bridge.'

Richard's lieutenant nodded,

'Aye, Sir Richard. I'll spring the trap as planned if you don't make it back in time, then we'll rendezvous with you later at the lagoon.'

Richard offered his hand, 'Good luck and may God be with you, William.'

Eagerly clasping his Captain's hand, William Howard's face was grave. Soberly, he whispered,

'May he watch over us all, Sir Richard.'

* * *

Relieved that no fresh tracks appeared on the mud, when the three men stumbled upon the Mayan track, Hendrik had been right. When Richard and Quinn first saw it, they marvelled at the size of the rope bridge spanning a two hundred-foot drop into the ravine below. Despite its great age, it was, as the Hollander had said, a wonder of engineering. Standing beside it, Quinn peered down into the dizzying depths of the gorge, and the rocks and fast flowing river far below. Absently, he picked up a stone and hurled it. All three men watched the stone disappear into the roaring, foaming waters.

Stepping back, Quinn awkwardly reached his broad hand back over his shoulder and grasped the axe he had carried from the Sea Hawk. He said in awe, 'It's certainly something to see, Master. Why, 'tis the most wondrous thing I've seen in the New World! It must have taken them savages a long, long time to build.' He sniffed with regret and rumbled, 'Shame we have to break it.'

187

Richard stared at the gently swaying bridge. Hardwood logs had been woven tightly together with jungle lianas to produce a sturdy walkway more than six feet wide, and at least a hundred paces long. The long wooden pathway was braced by a lattice of thick vertical lianas tied together, suspended from two stout ropes ten feet above his head. The rope supports were anchored to a solid wooden framework of thick logs, firmly braced and secured into the ground at either end of the bridge.

Richard stepped tentatively onto the bridge. It creaked and swayed slightly as it took his weight. He cautiously stepped forward, grasping one of the vertical lines for support, and jumped up and down several times; each time he felt the bridge shudder slightly as he landed. Turning back to the others, he declared,

'Seems sturdy enough to carry plenty of weight, but we don't have much time to bring it down.' Richard stared up at the formidable horizontal ropes above and below him. They were braided into the thickness of a man's leg, to support the great Mayan suspension bridge.

Richard walked back onto solid ground and spoke to his servant, 'Best climb up and start cutting one of the top ropes, Quinn.'

Quinn acknowledged his orders with a curt nod. Walking back to the furthest angled log, he stepped up and balanced himself. With arms outstretched, Quinn began cautiously, taking little sliding steps to inch his way up the sloping log. Richard turned to Hendrik,

'We'll start cutting the bottom ropes, but judging by their girth; it's going to take some time to sever them.'

Hendrik reached across his body, and drew his dagger. Running his thumb along its edge, he glanced suspiciously down at the bottom set of braided ropes. With resignation, he said with a sigh,

'You're right; this is going to take quite a while.'

188

Above them, Quinn reached the top of the supports. He stared down at one of the main ropes directly below his feet. He wore a deep frown upon his face. Balanced precariously as he was, even with his feet braced as best he could on the curving logs, it would be difficult to swing the axe and chop through the rope without slipping, and being pitched headfirst into the roaring chasm below. He shrugged to himself. Lowering the axe and resting it at his feet, he spat on his hands and then rubbed them vigorously together. Picking up the axe again, he hefted it over his head and took a first, cautious half-swing. As he did so, his two companions below began to saw at the thick bottom ropes.

Licking his dry lips, Quinn tasted the salty sweat which trickled down his face. As he suspected, the rope was proving difficult to cut. Having been steadily chopping for nearly ten minutes, he was only three-quarter of the way through the first rope. Below, Richard and Hendrik were struggling to part the woven fibrous strands. Richard was less than halfway through. He glanced over at Hendrik's efforts. The Hollander was also struggling at about the halfway mark. Richard straightened his aching back with a grunt, and called up to his servant.

'How close are you Quinn, how much longer?'

Quinn stopped for a moment to catch his breath. Wiping his big hand across his face, he looked down and replied,

'Another ten minutes, and I should be done on the first rope, master.'

Richard acknowledged the news with a nod. Disappointed with their slow progress, he glanced down at the Hollander opposite him and said,

'Might be a good idea to come over here and help me with this side, Hendrik. Together, we should part it at about the same time as Quinn finishes with the first rope above us.'

189

Blowing on the blister which was rapidly forming on the palm of his hand, Hendrik nodded and stood up. After stepping across, he crouched down in silence opposite Richard, and in the oppressive heat of the jungle, began to saw vigorously at the stubbornly resisting rope.

* * *

Will Howard had placed the crew of the Hawk carefully, when they reached the Mayan trail. Under Richard's orders, he had placed men in a long linear ambush, leaving small groups of his men hidden behind the jungle vegetation, covering several hundred paces along the trail. They had orders not to fire until he gave the word.

Listening to the buzzing insects around him, he started suddenly from his own concealed position beside the ancient Mayan track. Beyond the normal sounds of the jungle, he was sure he had heard something out of the ordinary. He tuned his head to one side, straining to identify the incongruous noise. Beside him, the Hawk's coxswain also heard something odd. Will Howard placed his finger to his lips and whispered,

'I hear animal bells. It must be the mule-train,' He stared gravely at the coxswain. 'Pass the word down the line. Warn the men, and tell them to make ready…'

* * *

Concealed by the jungle, hidden more than a mile away down the Mayan track, Quinn was, at last, close to parting the thick rope between his feet. Breathing heavily with his exertions, he puffed out his ruddy cheeks with relief that the task was almost done. Only a knot of straining fibrous strands remained; a few more blows with the heavy axe, he thought, should see them finally parted. Peering down at the two men crouched

190

below; Quinn could see that their rope was also close to being cut through. He was about to call down a warning but stopped suddenly. Over on the far side of the bridge, something caught his eye. Intrigued, Quinn lifted a hand to his brow, shielding his eyes from the sun's bright glare. He stared at the point where the far end of the track disappeared round a bend in the jungle. Sun suddenly glinted brightly again on something metal.

Whatever it was, it was still some hundreds of yards away, but as he stared, he slowly crouched down. Concern growing every moment at what he thought he saw, Quinn hissed a warning down to Richard and Hendrik. Urgently, he pointed over to the other side of the swaying bridge,

'Master! Look there, over on the other side...I, I think somebody's coming!'

* * *

Don Rodrigo swotted at something unseen, buzzing around his face. As the insect flew away, he felt a surge of relief when he saw the distant, shimmering outline of the rope suspension bridge. In the hours after dawn, his small column of cavalry had been forced to walk most of the fourteen miles from far off Veracruz, along the near impassable track. The Governor cursed the Mayans silently as he glanced over his shoulder at his men, who followed, heads drooping, in sullen silence. Despite his almost constant threats, their pace had slowed yet again. Beneath sweltering iron helmets, weighed down with heavy armoured chest and back plates, his men and horses were hot, tired and thirsty.

Forced by the terrain into leading their reluctant mounts on foot, the cavalrymen's strength had gradually ebbed during the morning, tormented as they were by the humidity, and being without the benefit of the shade of the jungle's canopy. The sun's cruel, unrelenting heat had taken its toll.

191

The bridge, Don Garcia decided, would make an ideal place to stop, find shade and rest, as the sun was fast approaching its hottest period during the hours straddling mid-day. In civilised Spain, of course, all sensible men stopped work and took the traditional siesta to sleep away the heat. Don Garcia had had enough of the temperature and the attention of ever attending flies. They would stop at the bridge; he decided. His men would erect a shaded shelter for him, and then look to themselves. Once rested, the column could push on until darkness. With luck, he thought grimly, and the blessings of the holy Saints, they would encounter the mule-train and its valuable cargo, well before nightfall. Thoroughly sick of the mission already, the Governor decided overall, it was a good plan to call a halt and stop on the far end of the bridge.

Quinn was still at the top of the log structure. He had come down out of his crouch, and was now lying flat on one of the thickest trunks, watching the slowly approaching Spanish column.

'Well!.. What's happening, Quinn?' Richard demanded impatiently.

Above the muffled roar of the cascading water deep in the gorge, Quinn called down,

'Definitely cavalry, master. Must be about twenty or so I think. They're moving very slowly, and I can't tell for sure, but I don't think they've seen us.'

Richard growled to himself with frustration. Another few minutes and they would have dropped the bridge. Now, if they moved, the Spanish would certainly see them.

He was about to reply to Quinn, when a ragged barrage of musket fire suddenly echoed from the hills behind him.

Hendrik's eyes widened. With a savage grin he said, 'The mule-train; Sir Richard. They've sprung the ambush!'

Despite his pleasure that Will and his crew were hopefully overwhelming the mule-train, Richard snorted. 'Yes, but look over there! The Spanish have heard the firing; they're coming at speed to rescue them.'

Hendrik looked across the bridge. Sir Richard was right; the Spanish horsemen were suddenly riding hard towards the bridge. The distant firing had swept away their lethargy, one group had broken away from the others, and were now charging towards them at the gallop.

Don Rodrigo had heard the gunfire too. It could mean only one thing; his precious mule-train was under attack. Furiously, he turned and snarled at the startled cavalrymen,

'Into your saddles, you lazy dogs!' He whirled to the officer in charge of the nearest troop, 'Take your men across the bridge. Secure the other side while I bring the others over.'

The captain saluted and shouted a series of rapid orders. Now in their saddles, he drew his sword. As he dug his spurs into his horse's flanks, the cavalry captain urged six of his mounted troopers forward,

'First section, at the gallop, follow me!'

Richard saw the horsemen charge. It could mean only one thing; they were coming across the bridge. Frantically, he yelled up at his giant servant,

'Quinn!...For the love of Christ man, cut the rope!'

The Cornishman didn't need to be told twice. He inched his way backwards and carefully stood up. Taking a last glance at the fast approaching cavalry, hurling a defiant, sulphurous curse towards them, he swung the axe as the first horseman clattered onto the bridge.

In that same moment, the Spanish officer leading his section spotted movement at the opposite end of the bridge. He clearly saw several white men darting about. Mouth suddenly dry

193

as a desert, he guessed their purpose, and the deadly danger he was suddenly in. Committed at a full gallop, approaching halfway across with his men close behind him, there was no time to rein-in and stop the charge. Frantically, he dug his spurs into his horse's sides to urge it to greater speed, before the swaying bridge fell.

With the drumming of hooves echoing in their ears, Richard and Hendrik were crouched down, sawing for all they were worth. Above them, there was a loud thud and an ear-splitting twang as Quinn's axe chopped through the last strands which held the bridge in place. Under the huge weight of the bridge, and the armoured horsemen who were frenetically charging across it, Quinn final stroke, and the massive tension on it, caused the thick support rope to hiss through the air as it snaked back past the thundering horses towards the opposite side.

Kneeling below Quinn, Richard stabbed feverishly at the last strands. The weight on the bridge was too great. With a loud crack, the last shards of the support rope snapped as one, and flew away across the chasm.

In the deadly race, the Spanish officer's hope had surged for a fleeting moment, He had nearly reached the opposite side when the walkway beneath his horse's flying hooves suddenly yawed violently and dropped away. With a desperate scream, the captain knew he was doomed. His horse pitched sideways and fell towards the crashing, churning waters far below. Unable to check his momentum, the captain followed. Behind him, five of his men fell like their officer, screaming their own terrified horrors; tumbling pell-mell with their flailing horses through the empty air of the deep chasm. Seeing his comrades' fall, the last rider pulled desperately on his reins, in a vain attempt to stop his own horse before it too clattered onto what little was left of the collapsing bridge. Sensing the danger, the snorting horse dug its hooves into the soft loam of the ancient Mayan track, but it was too late. In a swirling cloud of dust and flying stones, both horse and rider disappeared over the edge, in one final, stomach-churning moment.

As the swirl of dust and last cries of terror faded, a chilling silence enveloped the men on both sides of the chasm. Confused and overcome with shock, the remaining Spanish cavalrymen reined in their tired mounts. Some dismounted, and several crossed themselves and clasped small crucifixes they wore about their necks. In shock, they looked helplessly towards the Governor, who sat stunned in his own silver laced saddle. Don Rodrigo stared for a moment at the remains of the bridge, which now hung in tatters, silent and useless before him. His eyes followed the one remaining rope to the far side of the chasm. Something caught his eye. Was he mistaken, he wondered, or did he see something move over there? Assuming the bridge had failed under the combined weight of his men and their horses, blinking away the dust and tiredness from his eyes, Don Rodrigo tapped his spurs lightly against his horse's flanks. His mount responded instantly, and began to walk forward towards the edge of the chasm

Richard watched the last cavalryman fall. He felt no pleasure watching the man die. Under the secret orders of his Queen, he was waging war on the Spanish, and men died in war.' Hidden from view behind the logs, he motioned Hendrik back towards the cover of the jungle, just yards behind them. He looked up. Quinn had dropped down as soon as he had severed the rope, and was lying watching the horsemen on the other side.

'Quinn,' Richard hissed, 'Keep low and crawl back down here. We'll leave our enemies to their confusion and head straight back to the Hawk...'

195

Quinn heard his master, and immediately began to inch backwards, but suddenly, he froze. Straining his sharp eyes, he stared over the yawning chasm at the lone rider walking his horse towards its far edge. Staying flat, the Cornishman rubbed his eyes and stared again. He shook his head, unwilling to believe what his eyes told him.

Seeing his servant stop suddenly, Richard hissed again,

'Quinn, what's the matter? Come on man, we must away.'

Richard's manservant slowly turned his head, and stared down disbelievingly at his master. Grasping for the words, he called down softly,

'In God's name it's him, master! Over there…look! It's that Spanish bugger who shot Mistress Miriam!'

Chapter Twenty-Four

In that one, terrible moment, Richard started, as if his face had been slapped. His heart began to hammer in his chest. Cheeks flushing with terrible anger, his mind whirled as he struggled to take in what Quinn had just declared. Consumed and suddenly blinded with mindless, burning rage, Richard leapt to his feet and swept his sword from its scabbard.

Quinn saw his master jump up, and realised, to his horror, the awful hurt and mindless fury which had festered in Sir Richard's heart since Malta, had suddenly exploded. He cried out, as he began to slither down the thick log on which he had been lying,

'Master...*No!*'

Richard didn't hear his servant's desperate cry as he began to walk forward. Burning with insane rage, he stared unblinking across the chasm. There were other horses and riders milling around behind him, but only the weasel face of Don Rodrigo Salvador Torrez held his stare. Memories of his beloved Miriam's face and flashes of the bloody fighting on the walls of Malta flooded his raging mind. Richard remembered the Spanish nobleman's treachery, while the noise of the cascading water below was drowned out by the roaring of blood, which pounded in Richard's ears.

He saw Torrez jerk his reins and stop abruptly, as Richard walked further into the open. Don Rodrigo gasped with surprise; he too recognised his hated adversary. It was the same Englishman who had thwarted his opportunity for glory on Malta, and now had shattered his grandiose plans of easy riches. It was he, who in just a few short days had brought the noble House of Torrez to the very edge of disaster.

It was Don Rodrigo, whose mocking voice broke the silence,

'So we meet again, Englishman,' he shouted. I thought it was you who has caused me so much trouble in the past few weeks… Damn your eyes!'

Richard's anger diminished slightly, as he slashed the air with his sword with frustration. His reply, in fluent Spanish, was a primordial snarl,

'And damn your black-hearted soul, you murdering Spanish scum! I would kill you in an instant, if I could reach you.'

Don Torrez laughed mirthlessly,

'Then it is as well, Englishman that you cannot.'

There was little point in simply sitting exposed to the full blast of the sun's heat, trading insults with a man who probably would kill him if he had the chance, Don Rodrigo thought. He deftly turned his horse and showed both his back and his contempt to his helpless, frustrated enemy. As Richard ground his teeth with bitter frustration and glowered across the chasm, the Governor of Veracruz stared down coldly at his troopers, who had been listening to the short exchange. Words slipped from his thin, sneering lips…

'Don't just stand there, you idiots…Shoot him!'

Realising the English on the other side were responsible for the catastrophe of the ruined bridge; eager to avenge their fallen comrades, the cavalrymen quickly reached for the carbines held in leather stirrup holsters strapped in front of their saddles.

Dropping to one knee, the soldiers pulled back the iron locks and cocked their weapons. Each one, in turn, took careful aim.

Unaware of the imminent danger, Quinn had dropped to the ground and with Hendrik beside him now stood beside Richard. Urgently, concerned at Sir Richard's lack of concern about his exposure, Hendrik grasped Richard's arm and said,

'We should leave this place, Sir Richard. We have stopped the Spanish, and there is nothing more we can....'

Suddenly, as both sides of the chasm reverberated to the boom of the first Spanish carbine, Hendrik cried out in pain and fell to the ground, clutching his groin. Richard and Quinn both ducked, as more echoes boomed and bullets whizzed past or kicked up dust in the ground around them.

The short-barrelled, smooth-bore carbines were designed to hit quarry at close range. Targets at more than one hundred paces were far beyond the notoriously inaccurate weapons, handled by even the most skilled of marksmen. The bullet had been aimed at Richard, but had missed and struck Hendrik instead.

His overwhelming anger suddenly forgotten, Richard grabbed Hendrik's shoulder by his shirt. Quinn did the same on the other side. Together, as Don Garcia cursed and his cavalrymen frantically re-loaded, the two Englishmen dragged the groaning Hollander backwards into the sanctuary of the jungle's dense vegetation.

The Governor of Veracruz fumed. He had clearly seen one of Starkey's companions fall under the fusillade of firing. Not the Englishman's idiotic red-haired servant who had disturbed his moment of revenge on Malta, but another, whose scarred face looked vaguely familiar. His anger at Starkey slipping through his fingers yet again boiled over. He screamed with frustration and aimed his tirade and several kicks at the dismounted cavalrymen, still frantically loading powder, or ramming home lead bullets,

'Keep firing, damn you!

Pausing just inside the treeline, behind the solid cover of a towering hardwood tree, Richard knelt down beside Hendrik. The Hollander's face was deathly pale; the crimson trail which led from the chasm bore silent testimony that he had already lost

199

a lot of blood from the smashed femoral artery at the top of his thigh. Despite the tight grip he had on the ugly wound, blood pulsed rhythmically through Hendrik's fingers, matched to the beat of his fluttering heart. Richard tore off his shirt and rammed it, tightly bundled, over Hendrik's bloody hand. It stemmed the flow a little, but both kneeling Englishmen had seen this type of gunshot wound in battle before. As Hendrik lay groaning with his eyes closed, Quinn looked up from the pooling blood beneath the Hollander's wounded leg and stared forlornly into his master's eyes. Silently, he shook his head. Richard sadly acknowledged the gesture. Both men knew the truth of it.

Hendrik's eyes fluttered open. Weakening rapidly as he continued to bleed into the jungle floor, with thoughts far away, glazed, unfocused eyes stared up at Richard as he said softly,

'I am done for; Sir Richard…There is nothing more you can do for me. Please… please grant me a last wish find my wife and children and see them safety in England,' Hendrik groaned aloud, his body suddenly wracked with a fresh wave of pain. Catching his breath as the pain subsided a little, his voice weaker than before, he gasped breathlessly,

'I…I beg you, Richard… Give me your sacred word as a noble knight, and…and the sworn enemy of the Phillip of Spain….'

Richard stared into the darkening shadows in the dying Hollander's good eye. He nodded slowly and sadly. It was much that was asked of him, to plunge into the very heart of occupied Holland, but Richard owed so much to the brave man who now lay dying before him. A debt of honour was owed from the difficult days behind them, and Hendrik was a good Christian, and had become a friend.

A monkey chattered noisily far above them, but Richard ignored it,

'Yes, Hendrik…I give you my word… I swear by all that is sacred I will find your family and see them to safety…'

Richard's words soothed Hendrik's last moments. The Hollander's expression relaxed. The pain floated gently away; a peaceful, contented smile fell across his scarred features in his last, fleeting moments. A sigh escaped softly from Hendrik's pale lips, as the spice merchant's head rolled limply to one side.

The two Englishmen stared down at their fallen comrade in silence until Quinn muttered gently,

'He's gone, Master.'

Richard sighed. Miserably, he looked up at Quinn and said,

'Another good man dead, at the hands of those cursed Spanish.' With another, deeper sigh, Richard stood up and looked towards the gorge, hidden from view by a few yards of jungle. There was only silence around them, the distant firing behind them had stopped.

'We'd best check that the Spaniards remain trapped on the other side of the gorge, and pose no danger to us.'

Quinn nodded, but heard bitter frustration grow in his master's voice.

'It is the cruellest twist of fate that I am so close, but cannot draw steel against that black-hearted swine, Torrez.' Angrily, Richard glared into the surrounding jungle, 'We'll go and take a quick look, then come back here. If all is well, we will have time to bury poor Hendrik. Only then, when we have done our Christian duty by him, can we make our way back to the Hawk, and see how the ambush went…'

201

Chapter Twenty-Five

'We caught the Spaniards absolutely cold, Sir Richard!'

Will Howard's eyes sparkled with triumph, as he stood on the sandy beach within the hidden cove and gleefully recounted the events surrounding his successful ambush on the mule-train to his Captain. Behind him, the crew had unloaded the first twenty heavy saddle packs that the line of braying mules carried. It took four of the sailors to lift each one of the treasure laden packs into the Hawk's small boats, which were busy crossing each other, as they ferried each load to the ship, still anchored safely close to the sandy shoreline.

'I'd ordered our musketeers to take down the officers, and some of the soldiers who guarded the mule-train first, Sir Richard; that was the trigger,' he shrugged, 'then, howling like devils, we charged them.' The Hawk's first officer smiled broadly, 'It was over too quickly; a few tried to fight us off, but most of them, including the muleteers, ran for their lives and fled into the jungle on the other side of the track.' His eyes glittered as he remembered, 'We didn't pursue them as some of the mules had bolted, what with the gunfire and yelling, but we chased after them and caught them all easily enough, and then led them back here.'

Richard nodded; Will Howard had done well. He enquired, 'Any casualties?'

Will Howard shook his head, but his smile lingered,

'No, Sir Richard, not from the ambush, but one of the men got too close and was kicked by a bad-tempered mule for his trouble.'

It was Richard's turn to smile, but Will Howard had something more serious on his mind to report,

'I had a message from the coxswain just before you returned, Sir Richard. He's getting worried by the extra weight aboard. With the silver already aboard, the Hawk is starting to sit a little low in the water.'

Richard nodded,

'England needs every ounce of gold we can give her, Will. We could bury some of the treasure, but it will take too long to sail home, and then return here, dig it up and then sail back to England again. That could take, perhaps eighteen months...' He shook his head gravely, 'No, we'll just have to risk it, and pray the repairs hold and we have a smooth, uneventful crossing.'

Richard's first officer nodded, his Captain was right. They both knew time was of the essence. If England was to be even close to being ready for the Armada, when it came, their Queen needed the money they carried to commission and build stout ships.

'Hurry the loading, Will. I want to sail with the evening tide, as close to nightfall as possible. Don Rodrigo will throw everything he can at us to recover the gold, and I want to be long gone before he sends out his hunters...'

* * *

Still in its scabbard, Don Rodrigo hurled his sword and belt against the wall of his office. They clattered noisily, and then fell onto the floor with a crash. Ignoring them, he stamped angrily towards his desk. Bitter tears of frustration and despair threatened to erupt as he pounded his fist against the desk's polished walnut top. In his fury, he violently swept an ornate silver inkwell, quills and a pile of papers onto the marble floor, and then kicked at them savagely. Bitterly, he remembered the shaman's curse, but dismissed it. They were not the devil's dark magic, just a dying savage's last words. It was that bastard Englishman, Starkey, he fumed, he was to blame; everything was his fault. The swine had captured the Santa Juliana, and stolen six months' worth of silver from the mines to the north. He'd

203

destroyed valuable ships, and now, as a final insult had lifted the fortune carried by a hundred mules from under his very nose. On the verge of exploding, Don Rodrigo raised his fists and howled with rage. He sat for several minutes, as he tried to calm himself. He knew he must think of something, anything to save himself.

With the help of Bishop Acosta and his Inquisitors, the loss of the flotilla had been mitigated, and blame had been avoided, but now, within days, the mule-train was gone too. He would be recalled to Spain for sure, he thought, to answer for the huge losses he had suffered.

Don Rodrigo slumped into his chair, and sank his head into his hands. Now, there could be but one disastrous outcome. Both King and Church would blame him for everything; they would seize every ducat the Don had in his treasury to replace their own fat, and missing, percentages. There would be nothing left, no profits to pay the Don's creditors at home. He knew he was facing utter ruin.

Sinking into the depths of despair, he decided he must try to do something to mitigate this catastrophe. He would organise search parties to track down Starkey and find his cut-throat crew. Alvarez and that fat fool of an admiral must be set to work immediately. The Governor turned towards the doors of his office and roared,

'Fernadez!'

* * *

That night, as the sun set on a purple horizon, the heavily laden Hawk's sails unfurled as she slipped quietly from the hidden cove and began her first tack eastwards, towards the distant shores of England.

In the lengthening shadows, Richard lent against the guardrail alone at the bow, and breathed the salt air in deeply.

After the heat and claustrophobia of the jungle, it felt good to enjoy the true freedom of the open seas, and feel again the gently rolling deck beneath his feet. He still felt the bitter ache of frustration; Torrez had escaped his justice for a second time. Richard comforted himself with the thought that fate had thrown them together, once again, in the New World, and he felt in the depths of his bones that it would not be the last time he crossed the path of the Spanish Don. Next time, he thought, whatever happened, he would make an end of it.

Richard stared up at a seagull, as it wheeled and dived through the air, leading the Hawk out to sea. The skies above were clear, but Richard knew the dark clouds of war were slowly brewing over England and soon, his country's very existence would be in deadly peril, once King Phillip got his wish, and the great Armada set sail from Spain.

When the contents of his overloaded hold was safely carried over the mighty Atlantic, and delivered into the hands of his Queen, he would beg her indulgence of time to fulfil his promise to Hendrik. There would be great danger in going to occupied Holland of course, but he had given his solemn word, and he would rather die, than break it.

Richard heard footsteps behind him. It was his faithful servant, Quinn,

'Beggin pardon, master, the cook says supper's ready.' Quinn grinned, 'He says it's one of his specials….We're having cutlet of mule…'

Richard nodded with a half-smile,

'Thank you, Quinn. I'll be along shortly.'

Richard turned back, and stared into the gloom of the approaching night for just a moment longer. With a freshening wind in his face, some things were certain, in a dark and uncertain future. The Spanish Armada would come one day, nothing would stop that now. The few short years preceding their massed arrival may well fill his life with deadly peril, but his

205

undying thirst for vengeance, somehow, he swore silently to the four winds, would be fulfilled.

The End

Also by David Black

Siege of Faith

The Chronicles of Sir Richard Starkey #1

Far to the East across the sparkling waters of the great Mediterranean Sea, the formidable Ottoman Empire was secretly planning to add to centuries of expansion. Soon, they would begin the invasion and conquest of Christian Europe.

But first, their all-powerful Sultan, Suleiman the Magnificent knew he must destroy the last Christian bastion which stood in the way of his glorious destiny of conquest. The Maltese stronghold... garrisoned and defended by the noble and devout warrior monks of the Knights of St. John of Jerusalem...

A powerful story of heroism, love and betrayal set against the backdrop of the cruel and terrible siege of Malta which raged through the long hot summer of 1565. The great Caliph unleashed a massive invasion force of 40,000 fanatical Muslim troops, intent on conquering Malta before invading poorly defended Christian Europe. A heretic English Knight - Sir Richard Starkey becomes embroiled in the bloody five month siege which ensued; Europe's elite nobility cast chivalry aside, no quarter asked or mercy given as rivers of Muslim and Christian blood flowed...

Published on Amazon in Kindle Format & Paperback.

http://www.davidblackbooks.com

Also by David Black

Playing for England

What drives a man even to want to join the reserve SAS? -
The famous British Special Forces Regiment whose selection
process boasts more than a 90% failure rate.

David Black's book - Playing for England gives the reader
a fascinating first-hand insight into the rigours of the selection
and training process of those few men who earn the privilege of
wearing the SAS Regiment's sandy beret and winged dagger cap
badge.

Published on Amazon in Kindle Format & Paperback.

http://www.davidblackbooks.com

Also by David Black

EAGLES of the DAMNED

It was autumn in the year AD 9. The summer campaigning season was over. Centurion Rufus and his battle-hardened century were part of three mighty Roman Legions returning to the safety of their winter quarters beside the River Rhine. Like their commanding General, the Centurion and his men suspected nothing. Little did they know, but the entire Germania province was about to explode...

Lured into a cunning trap, three of Rome's mighty Legions were systematically and ruthlessly annihilated, during seventy-two hours of unimaginable terror and unrelenting butchery. They were mercilessly slaughtered within the Teutoburg, a vast tract of dark and forbidding forest on the northernmost rim of the Roman Empire.

Little could they have imagined, before they were brutally cut down, their fate had been irrevocably sealed, years earlier, by their own flawed system of provincial governance, and a rabid traitor's overwhelming thirst for vengeance. But how could such a military catastrophe have ever happened to such a well trained and superbly equipped army? This is their story...

http://www.davidblackbooks.com

Also by David Black

The Great Satan
Shadow Squadron #1

In The Great Satan, the first of his compelling new Shadow Squadron series, author David Black has produced his own fictional nightmare scenario: What if the Iraqi weapons that were said to be dismantled in the late 1990s included the ultimate WMD? And what if the deposing of Saddam Hussein left one of his most ruthless military leaders still at large, and actively seeking a customer for Iraq's only nuclear bomb?

Published on Amazon in Kindle Format & Paperback

http://www.davidblackbooks.com

Also by David Black

Dark Empire
Shadow Squadron #2

In the second of the thrilling SAS Shadow Squadron series, Sgt. Pat Farrell and his men are back in action, in DARK EMPIRE.

Pat and his reserve SAS troop are on a training mission in Kenya, when they are suddenly ordered into the heart of Africa, on what should be a straightforward humanitarian rescue mission.

Unfortunately, nothing is straightforward on the Dark Continent. Pat and his men quickly find themselves trapped, deep inside the primitive, war-ravaged Congo. Hunted by Congolese government forces and a savage legion of drug-crazed guerrillas, things don't always go to plan...even for the SAS!

Published on Amazon in Kindle Format & Paperback.

http://www.davidblackbooks.com

COMING SOON!

Also by David Black

The Devil's Web
Shadow Squadron #3

Al Qaeda have been quietly potting their revenge, after the death of their spiritual, Saudi-born leader, Osama Bin-Laden. A simple bombing or assassination won't do in the eyes of Zahira Khan, Pakistan's sinister chief Al Qaeda facilitator and planner. Hate-filled and utterly ruthless, he has devised something terrible – Al-Amin (the faithful), which will rival or perhaps even exceed the '*Spectacular*' 9/11 attack on New York's Twin Towers.

Can Sgt Pat Farrell and his reserve SAS Troop do the impossible, and thwart this diabolical plot, before acts of unspeakable horror are committed by men who welcome death?

The Devil's Web – Exclusive to Amazon and CreateSpace-
To be released in Kindle and paperback…*soon!*

http://www.davidblackbooks.com

Bruce County Public Library
1243 Mackenzie Rd.
Port Elgin ON N0H 2C6

CPSIA information can be obtained at www.ICGtesting.com
Printed in the USA
LVOW05s0027200315

431250LV00024B/652/P